CAN TIMMY SAVE TOYLAND?

Vincent McDonnell

The Collins Press

Published in 2005 by
The Collins Press
West Link Park
Doughcloyne
Wilton
Cork

© Vincent McDonnell 2005

First published in 1996 by Relay Press

A Cataloguing-In-Publication data record for this book is available from the British Library

ISBN: 1-903464-86-2

Typesetting: The Collins Press

Font: Hoefler Text, 14 point

Cover design: Deirdre O'Neill

Printed in Ireland by Colour Books Ltd

1
A Slimming Carbuncle

Mister Carbuncle, the fattest, nastiest, ugliest man in the world, was growing thinner and thinner. Now when he stared at his shadow on the wall of his prison cell, it no longer resembled a giant round football. Instead it looked like a duck egg that had grown legs and arms and a mop of hair.

Mister Carbuncle was wasting away. For six months now he'd been in prison and only had porridge to eat. This wasn't tasty warm porridge made with milk and sweetened with sugar. This was cold, thick, lumpy porridge made with water and salt.

Mister Carbuncle hated porridge. He had to screw up his face and hold his nose before he could eat it. Afterwards it lay on his stomach like a lump of lead and made him belch. But he was very ill mannered. He never put his hand before his face when this happened. Instead he rubbed his belly and burped and burped.

Once Mister Carbuncle had been the most feared man in the world. He'd been Boss of The Underworld and had lived in The Thieves' Den. He'd been very rich but he'd also been very greedy. He'd wanted more and more gold and jewels. So his adviser, Mister Illegal, a crooked lawyer, had devised a plan to kidnap Santa Claus and take over Christmas. But the terrible plan had been thwarted by a boy called Timmy Goodfellow. Mister Carbuncle and his thugs had been sent to prison. The gold and jewels had been taken from him and given to the poor.

In prison Mister Carbuncle thought of little else but gaining his freedom and having revenge on Timmy Goodfellow and Santa Claus. After that he was going to treat himself. He'd decided he would take over an ice-cream factory and eat nothing but ice-cream for a whole week. He'd start with huge bowls of vanilla flavoured ice-cream. Then he'd try strawberry and raspberry and pineapple before finishing up with a dozen more bowls of his favourite chocolate-flavoured variety.

Then Mr Carbuncle would pour gallons of vinegar into the cream. For months there would only be vinegar

2

flavoured ice-cream and all the children would be miserable and unhappy, their faces screwed up as they licked their cones. Only then would they realise how much he had suffered, eating the salty, lumpy porridge.

Thinking of this made Mister Carbuncle happy for a moment. He sat on his hard narrow bed and began to dream of the terrible tortures he'd inflict on Timmy Goodfellow and Santa Claus.

Just then someone approached his cell. The heavy steel door swung open and a warder ushered Mister Illegal inside. Because he was a lawyer he'd known how to plead in court and so hadn't been sent to prison. Today Mister Illegal had been in court to plead for the release of his Boss. He'd come straight from the court and was wearing his lawyer's long black gown and white curly wig.

As Mister Illegal entered the cell Mister Carbuncle eagerly leapt to his feet.

'Well?' he demanded. 'Am I to be released?'

'I'm afraid not, sir,' Mister Illegal cringed. 'The judge has ordered you must never be released.'

'Never,' Mister Carbuncle whimpered. 'Ne ... never.' He was so shocked that he flopped down on the bed. Tears sprung to his eyes. But his heart was as cold and as hard as steel and the tears were merely of rage and anger.

He leapt to his feet again and shouted at Mister Illegal.

'You're a fool,' he screamed. 'An idiot. A blathering ass. I'll ... I'll ...' But he couldn't think of any suitable punishment.

'Ye ... yes, sir,' Mister Illegal mumbled. 'If you say so, sir. I'm ... I'm all of those things.'

'I must get out of here,' Mister Carbuncle wailed. 'I'm wasting away. I want ice-cream. I must have ice-cream.'

'Ple ... please, sir,' Mister Illegal stammered. 'I ... I brought you ice-cream.'

'Ice-cream!' Mister Carbuncle's eyes lit up. 'Why didn't you say so? Where is it? Give it to me.'

'It's in my pocket,' Mister Illegal said. 'I had to hide it from the prison guards.' He put his hand in his pocket where his fingers encountered a wet, sticky mess. The day was hot and the ice-cream had melted. Mister Illegal cringed in horror. What was he going to do?

'Well then?' Mister Carbuncle demanded. 'Give it to me.' His stuck out his tongue and made licking movements.

'I ... I can't,' Mister Illegal said, his eyes wild with fear. 'It's melted. You'll have to go without.'

But Mister Carbuncle was crazy with his desire for ice-cream. He leapt at Mister Illegal and stuck his hand in the lawyer's pocket. He scooped out the runny ice-cream and lapped it up. It dribbled down his chin and up his arm. Then

4

Mister Carbuncle tried to stick his tongue in the pocket and lick up what remained. But the pocket was too deep.

Mister Carbuncle now ripped the pocket and exposed the lining. He turned it inside out and licked the ice-cream like a cat lapping milk. When it was gone he stuck the lining in his mouth and sucked it.

'Lovely,' he moaned. 'Oh it's lovely ... lovely ...'

At last there was no more ice-cream left and Mister Carbuncle pulled away. The dye from the lining had run and his face was streaked black.

'I want more,' he wailed. 'I must have more.' He stuck his hand in Mister Illegal's other pocket and scooped out what was there.

But in this pocket Mister Illegal kept the white powder he used to dust his wig. Mister Carbuncle scooped a great fistful of powder into his mouth. Some of it went up his nose and tickled him. He sneezed and blew the powder into Mister Illegal's face.

'Ah!' he shouted, jumping back. He was partly blinded and had to rub his eyes to clear them.

'Serves you right,' Mister Carbuncle sneered. 'That'll teach you to let me down. Now tell me how you're going to get me out of here. I must get out or I'll waste away. There'll be nothing of me left at all.'

'I'm thinking of a plan,' Mister Illegal said, squinting because there was powder in his eyes.

'And what's this plan?' Mister Carbuncle demanded.

'Oh, it's still secret,' Mister Illegal mumbled. 'There are lots of details to work out.' He cringed in a corner, frightened that Mister Carbuncle might realise he was lying, for Mister Illegal had no such plan. He couldn't admit that though.

'Well, what are you waiting for then?' Mister Carbuncle demanded.

'Waiting?' Mister Illegal whimpered.

'Yes. Waiting,' Mister Carbuncle roared. 'Why aren't you dealing with those details? I'm giving you a week to get me out of here. If you fail me I'll ... I'll make you eat your wig on your next visit.'

'Oh,' Mister Illegal whimpered again, fearfully. He touched his wig and thought of all the chewing he'd have to do. And he was certain the wig was infested with all sorts of creepy crawlies.

'Details,' he mumbled now. 'Yes, I must see to the details.' He bowed to Mister Carbuncle as he would to a judge in court and backed out of the cell.

Only when he was outside the great gates of the prison did Mr Illegal relax. But his relaxation was short lived. He still had to think up a plan to free his Boss. He had a week to do so otherwise Mister Carbuncle would carry out his threat.

Again Mister Illegal touched his wig and shuddered. Even if it were boiled for a whole day it would still take him hours to eat it. Mister Illegal hung his head and hurried along. As he rounded a corner he saw a group of unruly schoolboys.

'Get your hair cut,' they shouted gleefully. 'Is your name curly? That's a nice dress you're wearing.'

The taunts angered Mister Illegal. He swung about and most of the boys scampered to a safe distance. But one boy didn't. He was a small boy with blonde hair. He reminded Mister Illegal of someone.

Timmy Goodfellow! The name leapt to Mister Illegal's mind. That horrible boy who'd ruined everything. Mister Carbuncle would make him pay for that if he ever got out of prison. But would he ever get out? That possibility again made Mister Illegal think of the wig.

But maybe he wouldn't have to eat it. Mister Illegal smiled to himself as a plan to free Mister Carbuncle came to him.

'That's it,' he said to himself. 'That's how I'll get the Boss out of prison. It's a perfect plan. It's lucky for me that Timmy Goodfellow is so popular in the city. The authorities will readily agree to my demands.'

Satisfied that he wouldn't have to eat his wig after all, Mister Illegal walked on. By the time he reached The Thieves' Den he had his brilliant plan to free Mister Carbuncle all worked out.

2
A Worried Santa

Santa Claus was a worried man. His usual happy face was creased with deep lines. His blue eyes, normally sparkling like stars on a frosty night, were dulled, for he'd just received the terrible news that Toyland was in peril.

Toyland consisted of thousands of acres of ice. Built on the ice were the workshops where the elves made the toys. Here also were the huge warehouses where the toys were stored, along with the houses in which the elves lived. The cosy cottage where Santa Claus lived and the stables for the reindeer stood nearby. Now they were all in grave danger.

The ice was melting. Slowly, ever so slowly, Toyland was being destroyed. If Toyland disappeared there would be no more toys, no more Santa Claus and no more Christmas.

The world would become a place of misery and sadness.

As he sat at the table in his cottage, Santa picked up the report which he'd just been given by Elf Physics, his scientific advisor. Again Santa studied the figures supplied. According to the elf's calculation Toyland would soon disappear forever.

Santa Claus frowned and scratched his head. Then he turned to Elf Physics, who was perched on a corner of the table beside him. Elf Physics too was obviously worried and his furrowed face resembled a wizened red apple.

'This report is very worrying,' Santa Claus said. 'Can you tell me why Toyland is melting?'

Elf Physics nodded.

'As you know,' he said, 'the earth is heated by the sun. Now the sun is very hot. But here on the earth we are lucky because we have an atmosphere. This helps to keep the earth nice and cool so we're not cooked like meat in an oven.

'Part of our atmosphere consists of a layer of ozone gas. This keeps out much of the sun's harmful rays. But the ozone layer is being destroyed and more and more of those dangerous rays are allowed through. It is this that is melting the ice here in Toyland.'

'But what is destroying the ozone?' Santa Claus asked.

'Many, many things,' Elf Physics said sadly. 'Smoke from

factory chimneys; exhaust gases from cars, lorries and buses; coolants from faulty fridges and freezers; the gas that's used in aerosol sprays. All of these are destroying the ozone layer.'

'But this is terrible,' Santa said. 'What can we do to stop it?'

'We've tried many things,' Elf Physics explained. 'We've put out warnings but no one heeds them. The men who own the factories don't care. They just want to make more money. The men and women who drive the cars don't care. The people who throw out the faulty fridges don't care. The people who use the aerosols don't care.'

'But don't they have children?' Santa Claus asked. 'Don't they realise that if Toyland disappears, Christmas too will disappear? Don't they know that their children will be unhappy? Everyone knows that unhappy children make everyone else unhappy.'

'Adults don't think like that,' Elf Physics said, shaking his head. 'They're much too busy making money and trying to be successful. And then there are greedy men who would like to see Toyland destroyed. They know there is gold and oil and other precious minerals beneath the ice. They'd like to see Toyland destroyed so they could have those riches for themselves.'

Elf Physics stopped speaking and there was silence.

Only the crackling of the logs in the huge fireplace could be heard. Santa Claus always kept a good fire because he was a very old man and felt the cold. Santa rose from his seat and moved to the fire and sat in his favourite armchair. Elf Physics climbed down from the table and sat on the arm of the chair beside his friend. He could see Santa was worried and this made the elf sad.

'I must do something,' Santa said eventually. 'I'll write to the governments in every country in the world and warn them. I'll write to the presidents and the kings and queens. They'll take notice of me.'

'It would be no use,' Elf Physics said. 'They're only interested in being rich and famous. The don't care about Toyland.'

'But who cares then?' Santa Claus cried. 'Someone must care.'

'Only the children care,' Elf Physics sighed. 'But they have no power to change anything.'

'Oh, I don't know about that,' Santa Claus said thoughtfully. 'I think they might be the very ones to help us. In fact there is one admirable boy who'd definitely help us. And that boy is Timmy Goodfellow. I must get a message to him immediately. What would be the quickest way of doing just that?'

'It's very awkward getting from Toyland to the outside world,' Elf Physics warned. 'There's so much ice. And the ocean is so vast and treacherous.'

'What we need is a bird,' Santa Claus said. 'A bird could fly across the ice and across the ocean.'

'A snow goose,' Elf Physics said excitedly. 'I know the very one. Her name's Snowy. She's the best flyer I know. She's been farther south than any other goose in the arctic.'

'Summon her,' Santa Claus ordered. 'We've no time to lose.'

'Right, Santa,' Elf Physics nodded. 'I'll see to it immediately.' He hopped off the arm of the chair and left the cottage.

Santa Claus stared into the flames and hoped he could save Toyland. He knew he could rely on Timmy Goodfellow to do his best. But this was an enormous task and maybe it would be too difficult, even for the courageous Timmy.

3
Katie's and Timmy's Day

It was the most important day in Timmy and Katie Goodfellows' lives. Today they would find out if Katie, who had been crippled in a road accident, would ever walk again.

Four weeks ago Katie had had an operation. Mister Surgeon had fitted steel pins in Katie's hips. Then both her legs had been enclosed in plaster. Now today the plaster would be removed. If the operation had been successful then Katie would be able to walk again.

Timmy was worried as he travelled to the hospital with his foster parents, Mister and Mrs Kindheart. He was hoping that Katie would be able to walk again. But Mister

Surgeon had not been able to guarantee that the operation would be a success.

As they sped through the city from Friendly Cottage, their limousine was accompanied by Mister Reporter and a television crew. Because Timmy had saved Christmas, he was now the most important boy in the city and everyone wanted to know if his sister would walk again. This was the biggest news event of the year and would be transmitted live to all parts of the world via satellite.

All over the world children and adults were gathered round their television sets, anxiously waiting for news. Women were nervously biting their nails while men were constantly running to the kitchen to make tea no one wanted.

But this anxiety was nothing compared to Timmy's. Only he knew how much his sister wanted to walk again. If the operation was not successful then Katie would be miserable for the rest of her life.

The limousine reached the hospital and swung in through the gates. A great crowd was gathered there who waved to Timmy.

'Good luck!' they shouted and fell silent.

The limousine drew up to the hospital entrance. Mister Porter rushed forward and opened the door. Timmy and his foster parents got out. Mister Surgeon was waiting for them.

He was clearly worried and kept fiddling with his stethoscope.

Mr Surgeon led them inside and they marched down a long corridor to Katie's ward. Mister Reporter and the television crew followed. As soon as Katie saw them her face lit up like a lamp.

'Now,' Mister Surgeon said, his voice trembling with apprehension, 'we will remove the plasters.'

Miss Nurse moved forward. In her hand she held a small electric cutting tool. She switched it on and the motor's buzz sounded like a wasp caught in a spider's web. Carefully Miss Nurse cut open the plasters while everyone held their breath. All around the world, in houses and hospitals, in hotels and factories, from north to south and east to west, people too held their breath.

When the plasters had been removed, Miss Nurse stepped back.

'Come on now, Katie,' Mister Surgeon said. 'Let's see if you can walk.'

Nobody moved. Katie stared from one person to another. There was fear in her eyes. She made an attempt to raise herself up but fell back again.

'I ... I can't,' she whispered. I'm ... I'm afraid.'

Mister and Mrs Kindheart stared at the black and white tiles on the floor. Mister Surgeon tapped the end of his

15

stethoscope and heard a sound like thunder in his ears. Miss Nurse examined the cutting tool. Mister Reporter fiddled with his microphone and Mister Cameraman adjusted his lenses.

All over the world women hid their heads in their hands. Men turned away and looked out of windows. They whistled and pretended they weren't upset. Still others rushed off to the kitchen again to make even more tea. Children sniffed and held back their tears.

Only Timmy Goodfellow looked at his sister with the salt prick of tears in his eyes. There was a lump too in his throat. But he knew he had to be brave for Katie. She needed him now.

He walked to the bed and took Katie's tiny hand in his.

'It's OK, Katie,' he said. 'I'm here now. I'll help you. Come on. You can do it.'

Slowly, with Timmy's help, Katie sat up. He held her arm as she swung her legs over the side of the bed.

'Easy,' Timmy said. 'I'll support you. Now slowly, let your feet touch the floor.'

Katie did as she was told. As the camera filmed the scene, Katie lowered her feet onto the floor. With Timmy's arm for support she gingerly stood up. She swayed and would have fallen if Timmy hadn't held her. 'I can't,

Timmy,' she cried. 'I'll never be able to walk.'

'Of course you will,' Timmy said bravely, holding back his tears. 'Now take a step. I won't let you fall, I promise.'

Katie took a faltering step. She stumbled but Timmy supported her. Then she took another step. Then another and another and another.

'Look,' she cried. 'I'm walking. I can walk again.'

A great cheer and a burst of applause erupted in the ward. By the door other nurses, doctors and patients had gathered. Now they all joined in the cheering and clapping.

All around the world people cheered. They grabbed each other and began to dance. All their fears and tensions fell away. Children began to jump and cheer.

Now Katie let go of Timmy's arm and took a couple of steps on her own. Her feet felt wobbly but she was careful. She walked across the ward and back again. Then she hopped across the ward and back. Then she skipped across the ward and back. Then she did a little dance. Everyone laughed and cheered.

Timmy Goodfellow watched his sister with tears of joy in his eyes. The television camera zoomed in on his face. He was so happy to see Katie walking again.

Meanwhile, in the matron's office, the telephone began to ring. It rang and rang as people called to give Katie and Timmy their best wishes. A girl came running to the ward door.

'Mister Mayor sends his best wishes,' she called.

Then another girl came running.

'Madam President sends her best wishes,' she said.

Another girl soon arrived. And another and another. They were running up and down the corridor outside. They were so excited, they even got the messages wrong. 'Madam Mayor sends her best fishes,' one called out. 'Mister Minister sends his best dishes,' cried another.

Everyone in the ward was laughing. All over the world people were laughing. There was so much excitement that the satellite couldn't cope. Twenty two thousand miles up in space it gave a bang and a whoosh and belched smoke. On earth all the television screens went blank.

It was just as well. People had been getting more and more excited. No one wanted to do any work. Children didn't want to go to school. Cars and buses had stopped in the streets. Air traffic controllers had tuned their radar sets to the broadcast. Now, as the screens went blank, people calmed down.

At the hospital normality returned. The telephone stopped ringing and people stopped rushing about.

Mister Surgeon led Katie and Timmy and their foster parents to their limousine. They got in and drove off.

18

The crowd was still waiting at the gate for a glimpse of Timmy and Katie. Now, as the limousine drove away, they waved and cheered.

'Hooray for Timmy and Katie,' they shouted.

Timmy and Katie waved back. Then the limousine turned the corner at the end of the street and was lost to sight. The crowd began to disperse. But their excitement hovered behind them at the gate like a huge cloud.

That morning one other person was watching television. But he didn't cheer once. As his screen went blank, Mister Illegal switched off the television. Then he sat back in his chair and began to think.

He had planned to kidnap Timmy Goodfellow and threaten to do terrible things to him if Mister Carbuncle and his gang weren't released from prison. But now Mister Illegal had a much better idea. Cackling, he took a pen and paper and began to draw up a new, more terrible plan.

4
The Snow Goose

Snowy was the best-known goose in the arctic. Her exploits were legendary. She had flown farther south than any bird and had encountered many dangers. And she had always returned to tell the tale.

Her home was the most popular place on the ice cap. It was there that the snow geese gathered, especially the younger ones who had never been south and the elderly ones who would never fly south again. They loved to sit around and listen to Snowy recount her exploits.

Snowy was telling of a particularly dangerous exploit to a captive audience when there was a commotion outside. A young goose rushed to the window and looked out.

'Why it's Elf Messenger from Toyland,' he honked.

'Something's wrong,' an old goose said in a worried honk. A hush descended on the gathering. They were all secretly concerned in case there was something the matter with Santa Claus. After all, he was getting quite old.

There was a knock and Elf Messenger entered. He was small and wizened and his wiry red hair, which resembled a pot scourer, peeped from beneath his knitted hat.

'I bring a message from Santa Claus,' he said to Snowy. 'He wishes you to undertake a mission on his behalf. He's asked me to stress to you that it may be dangerous.'

Snowy nodded gravely. She stretched her neck and tilted her head to one side. It was a dramatic and serious pose. But in reality her heart beat with excitement. Life had been getting dull lately and she yearned for adventure. And what was the use of adventure if there wasn't a little danger thrown in?

'I must go to Toyland immediately,' Snowy said. 'I'm afraid the story must wait until I return. But by then I may have a more exciting story to tell.'

A tremor of excitement rippled through the younger geese. They thought that adventure was what life was all about. They could hardly wait to have adventures of their own.

But the older geese grew quiet. They were very fond of Snowy and loved to hear of her adventures. But those adventures were over. They posed no danger anymore. This new adventure had not even begun though. There was no certainty they would ever see Snowy again.

With heavy hearts the older geese bade goodbye to their friend.

'Take care,' they said. 'Safe journey.'

But the younger geese gathered around honking excitedly.

'Wish we were going with you,' they chorused. 'Hope you have a really dangerous adventure.'

Snowy dipped her head in acknowledgement.

'I'll see you soon again,' she said. 'I'll have a great story for you.'

She looked around her home once more and then spread her wings and inspected them. She preened a feather here and there. But it was only from habit, for she kept her feathers, especially her flight feathers, in tip-top condition.

Everything was in order and she waddled outside onto the ice cap. Seeming clumsy and ungainly she waddled on, gathering speed, flapping her enormous wings faster and faster until she was airborne.

There is no more beautiful sight in the world than a snow goose in flight. Their feathers and down are of the purest white and they are the most graceful of flyers. Now Snowy dipped her wings in a last farewell and banked away. She honked, once, twice, a third time, and the sad sound echoed forlornly across the ice cap. A few moments later she was lost to sight.

Meanwhile, Mister Illegal was making progress with his plan to free Mister Carbuncle. The lawyer realised he would need help and for this reason he visited the most disreputable part of the city.

Here the houses had no windows. Instead, timber planks were nailed over the openings. Doors were made from half-inch thick steel sheets. Mister Illegal hurried through the narrow mean street, glancing anxiously about him. He had dressed in his oldest suit and carried a briefcase he had found in the attic. He hoped that any thug who saw him would think he was poor and leave him be.

Mister Illegal was looking for a particular house. Eventually he found it down a narrow alleyway. He knew it was the house he sought because it had half-inch thick steel sheets over the windows as well as the door.

Mister Illegal rapped on the steel with his knuckles, which made him wince. Someone growled inside and Mister Illegal's heart skipped a beat. He was tempted to run away, but before he could gather up courage to do so, the steel door swung open.

The face of the man who leered out at him was twisted.

The nose was beneath the man's left eye while his mouth was directly beneath his right eye. His teeth were black and sharp and the top ones almost reached halfway down his chin. He was bald and had no eyebrows, but tufts of hair, like small black caterpillars, stuck out of his nostrils and his ears.

Mister Illegal couldn't speak. He couldn't move. He thought he had never seen anyone or anything as ugly before. He stood staring with wide-open eyes, his whole body trembling.

'What are you staring at?' the man demanded, and Mister Illegal's eyes popped in his head, for the man had a high-pitched voice. Each word was a squeak. Mister Illegal's lips opened and closed convulsively. But he made no sound.

At this, the ugly man's hand shot out and caught Mister Illegal by his lapel. The terrified lawyer was dragged into the dark hallway and the steel door clanged shut. A knife blade flashed in a ray of light coming through a chink between the door and the jamb.

'Explain yourself,' the man ordered. 'Otherwise, I'll slice you up.'

'P ... p ... please don't, Mister Savage,' Mister Illegal whimpered. 'I ... I need your help. You see, I work for Mister Carbuncle. I'm his lawyer. He's in prison right now but I'm planning to free him. I want you to help me.'

'At your service,' Mister Savage grinned. His face twisted even more but luckily it was dark and the lawyer couldn't see it clearly.

'I have a plan to free the Boss and his gang,' Mister Illegal went on. 'It involves kidnapping a girl called Katie Goodfellow. Once we've got her we'll threaten to make her suffer if the authorities don't comply with our demands.'

'I could break her arms,' Mister Savage said gleefully. 'One at a time, of course. A young girl's bones make a satisfying cracking sound. Or stamp on her toes. They make a pleasant squashing sound.'

'We'll have to see,' Mister Illegal said. He disliked violence. 'Maybe just one arm,' he added, to humour Mister Savage. 'And a couple of toes.'

'Big toes,' Mister Savage pleaded. 'They squash best of all.' He was clearly excited, and released his grip on the lawyer's lapel.

'Possibly,' Mister Illegal said. 'But I want you to kidnap her first and then guard her.'

'Guard her!' Mister Savage again caught the lawyer's lapel. 'Are you making fun of me?' he screamed in his high-pitched voice. 'I'm the most violent thug in The Underworld. Everyone's afraid of me. I'm not a babysitter. I eat babysitters.

I break arms and squash toes. And noses. And ears. Guarding a young girl is a job for an old woman.'

'Of course,' Mister Illegal mumbled. 'I'm terribly sorry. I realise such a job is beneath your comprehensive abilities. But I take it you don't regard kidnapping itself to be beneath your dignity?'

'Oh no,' Mister Savage said. 'I'd like that. I like to drag the victims by the hair. They scream most satisfactorily.' He released his grip once more.

'I'm sure they do,' Mister Illegal squirmed. 'Well, I'll be in touch when I require your undoubted talents. I must make other arrangements now. There's a woman I know – a Mrs Haggard – who'd be only too delighted to be a guard. I must go and see her.'

Mister Savage opened the steel door and Mister Illegal scuttled out. He was never more relieved to escape and he scampered away. Mister Savage watched him and laughed. Then he went back inside.

Mr Savage was delighted with the job offer and decided to get in some practice at breaking arms. He went out to his shed and spent an hour breaking timber. The sound was like music to his ears. It wasn't anything like the sound of the real thing though. Bones, he felt, were always so much better.

5
A Warning from Toyland

Snowy Goose had never been so far south before. The long journey across ice and ocean had drained her strength. Her wings beat slowly and ponderously but she was nearly there at last. Ahead she could see the city where Timmy Goodfellow lived.

Santa had given her directions to Friendly Cottage and Snowy was confident she would find it. She descended and began to seek out the landmarks she had been given. Flying from one landmark to another, she soon saw the crooked chimneys of Friendly Cottage.

Snowy came in low over the shelter belt of pine trees to land in the rear garden. Here Timmy and Katie were playing hide and seek, and as Katie ran about seeking her brother she saw the snow goose flop down on the grass. Katie immediately forgot her game and ran to the stricken bird. Going down on her knees, she stared into Snowy's eyes. Slowly she reached out and gently stroked the bird's long neck.

'Don't be frightened,' Katie said, soothingly. 'No one will harm you here.'

Snowy was still breathless from her ordeal and could only dip her head in acknowledgement.

'Don't try to speak,' Katie continued. 'I'll get you water and food. When you've got your breath back you can tell me what you're doing so far from home.'

Stroking the goose once more, Katie ran off to get water and food. Mrs Kindheart fed the birds that came into the garden and there was always birdseed in the house.

When Katie ran back with bowls of water and food, Timmy had emerged from his hiding place and was staring at Snowy in amazement.

'Where did she come from?' he asked his sister.

'I don't know,' Katie replied. 'The North Pole, I suppose.'

'I've never heard of one flying so far south before,' Timmy said. 'Maybe when she's had food and drink she can tell us what she's doing here.'

With that, Katie placed the bowls on the grass and she and Timmy watched the goose eat and drink her fill. Then

Snowy flexed her body and stretched out her wings.

'Thank you, Katie,' she said. 'And you too, Timmy. I was hungry and thirsty. It's been a long journey.'

Timmy's mouth hung wide open.

'How ... how do you know our names?' he mumbled.

'Know your names!' Snowy honked. 'Why there isn't a bird or animal from here to the North Pole who hasn't heard of you both. Didn't Santa tell us all about you.'

'You know Santa?' Timmy exclaimed.

'Of course,' Snowy answered. 'I was talking to him the other day. I ...' But with that the goose's head drooped and the sparkle that had come into her eyes dimmed somewhat.

'What's wrong?' Timmy asked. 'Is something the matter with Santa?'

'Oh no!' Katie exclaimed. 'Not Santa. He's ... he's not sick, is he?'

'Not sick,' Snowy answered quietly. 'But he's deeply troubled. You see Toyland is being destroyed. If something isn't done, then it will disappear forever. It's why I've come here. Santa sent me to seek your help.'

'I'll do anything I can,' Timmy said, his voice breaking. 'Anything ...'

'Me too,' Katie whispered.

'Santa knew you would,' Snowy said. 'Now let me tell

you everything I know.'

While Timmy and Katie lay on the grass, Snowy sheltered from the sun in their shadow and told her story. It was a long story and it took much time. When she had finished, Timmy and Katie lay in silence, thinking about what they had just heard. Eventually Timmy roused himself and sat up.

'We must let the whole world know what's happening,' he said. 'I'll contact my friend, Mister Reporter. He'll broadcast the story on television. People will then find out what's happening.'

'I'll help too,' Katie added. 'I'll threaten not to be happy ever again if people don't stop polluting the earth.'

'Santa made the right choice in picking you two to help him,' Snowy said proudly. 'If anyone can save Toyland, you two can.'

'There's no time to lose,' Timmy said. 'But first you must come inside out of the sun. I know the very place for you. Then tomorrow you can return to the North Pole and tell Santa we'll do our best to help him.'

With that the three made their way into the cottage, Snowy waddling between her two new friends. As they passed the sitting room door, Snowy honked in alarm, for inside, lazing on the arm of the easy chair, directly in the rays of the sun, was the cat, Mister Tom.

'Oh, don't mind him,' Katie laughed. 'Mister Tom won't hurt you. Even our friends Mousey Mouse and Ratty Rat aren't frightened of him. They even call to see him from time to time.'

Snowy nodded but nevertheless she kept close to Timmy as he led her into the kitchen.

'Here we are,' Timmy said. 'The very place for you. I'm sure you'll feel right at home.'

With that, he opened the door of the huge fridge. With Katie's help, he took the items from the bottom shelf and placed them elsewhere.

'Now Snowy,' he said, 'there's a home from home for you.'

'It's lovely and cool,' Snowy enthused, putting her head into the fridge. 'Just like on a warm day at home.'

'Did you say a warm day?' Katie asked, in disbelief.

Snowy honked and they all laughed. Then she climbed into the fridge and settled her wings about her. She tucked her head under one wing and was almost immediately fast asleep. Quietly Timmy pushed the door to until it was nearly closed. He was careful to leave a small gap open so Snowy could breath. Nodding to Katie, he made his way back out to the front garden where Mrs Kindheart was watering her roses.

Timmy asked if he could use the telephone and she gave him permission. He thanked her and went back inside. From the hall, he rang Mister Reporter. There was no time to lose.

6
The Latest Latest Show

Timmy and Katie Goodfellow were nervous as they waited at the rear of the television studio. In a few moments they would appear on The Latest Latest Show, the most famous one on television. Mister Presenter would interview them and the programme would be transmitted all over the world by satellite.

A rather stern woman stood beside them awaiting a signal.

'Follow me,' she said brusquely as she received the signal. 'Quickly now. Mister Presenter doesn't like to be kept waiting.'

Timmy and Katie hurried after her down a corridor. From up ahead they could hear the sound of applause. They turned a corner and saw an open door. The woman stood aside and Timmy and Katie passed through.

The glare of the lights made them blink as they entered the studio which was resounding with applause. A smiling Mister Presenter, the most famous man on television, shook both their hands and showed them to their seats.

Mister Presenter introduced them. Meanwhile Timmy and Katie stared at the lights and cameras and the many technicians and experts who helped the show run so smoothly.

Both were nervous and they stared at the audience, seeking a friendly face. As they scanned the rows of people they caught sight of their foster parents and breathed a sigh of relief.

Mister Presenter completed his introduction and then turned to Timmy and Katie.

'Now,' he said, 'can you tell me why Snowy Goose came to your home?'

'She was sent by Santa Claus,' Timmy answered, 'to warn us that the ice at the North Pole is melting. If it melts completely, Toyland will disappear and there will be no more Santa Claus or Christmas.'

'Why is that?' Mister Presenter asked.

'Because Toyland was given to Santa Claus by the Queen of the North,' Timmy explained. 'Santa helped her in a battle with the Wicked Witch and as a reward he was given Toyland. But it only belongs to Santa as long as the ice remains. If the ice melts, Santa loses his claim.'

'Ah,' Mister Presenter nodded. 'I see.'

'Santa is deeply disturbed by this,' Katie joined in. 'That's why he sent Snowy to warn us. It's his last desperate attempt to save Toyland.'

'This is serious,' Mister Presenter said. He scratched his ear and frowned. 'Can you tell me why the ice is melting?'

'It's due to pollution,' Timmy said. 'Pollution is destroying the ozone layer which protects the earth from the harmful rays of the sun. The earth is getting hotter and hotter and the ice is melting.'

'And what can we do to prevent this?' Mister Presenter asked.

'We must stop the pollution,' Timmy said. 'We must ensure that factories no longer emit harmful smoke and chemicals. We must ensure that cars, buses and lorries use petrol that doesn't harm the environment. We must use only fridges and freezers that have friendly chemicals as coolants. And, of course, we must use safer chemicals in aerosols.'

Mister Presenter smiled. But there was no trace of humour in his eyes.

'I understand,' he said, 'that your foster father owns a factory that makes aerosols. Why doesn't he stop polluting the atmosphere?'

At this a ripple of applause rang out in the audience. It made Katie angry and she turned to Mister Presenter.

'My foster father does own a factory that manufactures aerosols,' she said. 'But from next month on he will only use ozone-friendly products. They do no harm to the atmosphere at all.'

This drew loud applause from the audience. Mister Presenter realised that most people supported Timmy and Katie and, as always, he went with the wave of popularity.

'So what can be done,' he asked, 'to prevent this catastrophe?'

'Governments must stop the pollution,' Timmy said. 'They must pass new laws ensuring that factories don't emit harmful gases. They must ensure that all vehicles use clean petrol and have devices fitted to prevent exhaust fumes.'

'And everyone should buy ozone-friendly aerosols,' Katie added. 'And fridges and freezers that have friendly coolants.'

'I see,' Mister Presenter said. 'But will governments take action?'

'If they don't,' Timmy said with determination, 'then I'm going to call on all the children in the world to go on strike. We won't eat our greens or wash behind our ears.'

'Or clean our teeth or comb our hair,' Katie added.

'Or learn our tables or our spellings,' Timmy went on, gathering enthusiasm.

'Or cut our toe nails or pick up our clothes after us,' Katie put in.

'This is serious,' Mister Presenter said gravely. 'This is very serious indeed. I hope that Madam President, Mister Minister and Mister Mayor are listening and taking note.'

'I hope so too,' Timmy said. 'Otherwise there may be serious consequences.'

'I've no doubt of that,' Mister Presenter said. His worried face as he ended his show mirrored most of the faces in the audience. They were all coming to realise the seriousness of the childrens' threat to go on strike. It had never happened before and no one could really imagine what it would mean.

It was unheard of for children not to wash behind their ears. Who could know what might happen if they didn't do so? Would weeds sprout in the dirt? Or would worms and horrible slimy things crawl out? Farmers were worried about their greens. Would fields of cabbages rot away if the children refused to eat? And toothpaste manufacturers were wringing their hands at the thought of their products not being used anymore.

In government offices a hurried meeting was held

between Madam President and Mister Minister.

'We must do something,' Mister Minister said. 'If we don't the economy will be ruined. The people will vote me out and I'll lose my big car and my chauffeur and my mobile phone.'

'What about me?' Madam President wailed. 'I'm so busy I won't have time to pick up my children's clothes. They'll pile up to the ceiling and then some newspaper will publish pictures of it and I'll be ruined. I'll never be able to go out and face the public again.'

'We must consider legislation,' Mister Minister said, drawing a pad and pen towards him. 'There's no time to lose.'

While this was happening a man sat at a desk poring over books on law and old maps. Mister Illegal too had seen the television programme – he had watched it with ever increasing interest and excitement. When the programme was over he had switched off the television and gone into his library. There he sought out books and maps and took them over to his desk.

Soon he found what he was looking for. Timmy Goodfellow had been absolutely correct when he said Santa Claus would lose all rights to Toyland if the ice melted. In fact, when the ice melted, whoever had made a claim on Toyland would then own it. Not only that but they would own the rights to the oil and gold deposits which lay beneath the ice. With those the owner would become the richest man in the world.

Mister Illegal chortled at thoughts of his plan, and he rubbed his hands together. Then he took paper and a pen, and, with his face set determinedly, drew up a claim on Toyland on behalf of Mister Carbuncle. When the ice melted Toyland would belong to The Boss of The Underworld. Not only would he become the world's richest man, but he would also have sweet revenge on his most hated enemy, Santa Claus.

Mister Illegal realised it was time to put his plan to free his Boss into action. After stamping the paper to make it legal, he sent for Mister Savage.

'Tomorrow's the day,' Mister Illegal said, when Mister Savage arrived at The Thieves' Den.'

'I'll be ready,' Mister Savage growled. 'Now I must shave.'

'Do you need a razor?' Mister Illegal asked.

'Razor!' Mister Savage laughed. 'Razors are only for weaklings. I use this.' With that he took a pincers from his pocket and began to pluck the hairs from his face, one by one. 'Lovely,' he said. 'That's lovely.'

Mister Illegal groaned with fright. For a moment he was tempted to call the whole thing off. But then he remembered that Mister Carbuncle had threatened to make him eat his wig if he didn't get him out of prison. He would have to go through with it no matter what. Tomorrow Mister Savage would strike. And within 24 hours Mister Carbuncle would be free. Then, when the ice melted, he'd be rich and happy and Mister Illegal could relax again.

7
Savage Strikes

Snowy Goose left for the arctic at sunset the next day. 'Santa Claus will be delighted with the news,' Snowy told the children before she departed. 'You certainly managed to get all the governments of the world to bring in new laws to stop the pollution. At least now Toyland will be saved.'

'Tell Santa Claus we were delighted to be able to help,' Timmy said. 'And tell him we'll see him at Christmas.'

'I'm going to miss you terribly, Snowy,' Katie said, tearfully.

'Well, I for one won't be sorry,' Mister Tom said gruffly. 'I haven't had a decent cat nap since she arrived.' With that he settled himself on the arm of his chair and closed his eyes.

'Don't mind him, Snowy,' Katie said. 'He's just being his old grumpy self.'

At this everyone laughed and followed Snowy into the garden. She made a few adjustments to her feathers, ruffled her wings and with a hug from Katie, took to the air. She honked a final goodbye, then turned her head to the north and the cold wastes of the arctic.

Katie and Timmy watched until Snowy disappeared from sight. Katie rubbed her eyes and sniffed and Timmy was upset to see his sister so sad. He wanted to cheer her up.

'I'm going to meet my friend, Teddy Needy,' Timmy said, cheerfully. 'He's working at the funfair in the city. I promised to help him. Do you want to come with me? You might enjoy yourself there.'

'No thanks, Timmy,' Katie said. 'I'm going to stay here. I want to write about Snowy so I won't ever forget her.'

'I'll see you later then,' Timmy said, and, after telling his foster mother where he was going, he set off on the bus for the city. As the bus came to the city's outskirts, it stopped at traffic lights. Timmy stared down at the vehicles below him and saw a black van with dark windows. Through the windscreen he caught a glimpse of a face. It was the most savage human face he had ever seen and it reminded him of someone. Timmy shivered. Just then the lights changed and the bus pulled away. Timmy didn't see the van or the driver again.

Mister Savage sang as he drove along. The song was his favourite, about warts and boils and sores. It was the one he sang when he was happy. And he was happy today. He hadn't worked in a long time and it felt good to be working again.

Mister Illegal had given him directions to Friendly Cottage and Mister Savage followed the route. While stopped at traffic lights he saw a boy watching him from the top deck of a bus. His face seemed familiar but, before he could figure out who the boy was, the lights changed.

'I bet I scared him,' Mister Savage laughed. He was delighted when he scared people and he would have loved to have seen the look of terror on the boy's face. But the fear on Katie Goodfellow's face would do just as well.

Still singing, he drove on and soon reached Friendly Cottage. He parked the van down a narrow track and scrambled through a gap in the hedge into the garden. From here he ran to the rear of the cottage.

Because the day had been warm, the windows were open and through the one in the bathroom Mister Savage entered the cottage. From here he made his way to the hall and saw Mrs Kindheart preparing supper in the kitchen. On tiptoe he crept to the bottom of the stairs and stealthily climbed up to the bedrooms.

He found Katie's room and saw her writing at a desk. In three long strides he crossed the room, grabbed Katie and clamped a hand over her mouth so she couldn't cry out.

'Don't struggle or make a sound,' he hissed. 'If you do, I'll pull your hair out from the roots.'

Gripping her arm tightly, Mister Savage led her from the room and down the stairs. Here he checked the way was clear before he dragged her to the bathroom. He made her climb out the window and he dragged her across the garden towards the gap in the hedge.

They almost made it without anyone seeing them. But just then Mister Tom decided to go for a stroll. As he came out into the garden he spotted Katie and Mister Savage. Mister Tom let out a plaintive miaow and this brought Mrs Kindheart running to see what was wrong.

She was just in time to see Mister Savage drag Katie through the gap in the hedge.

'Oh no,' Mrs Kindheart wailed. She ran across the garden, calling out to Katie. But as she reached the hedge she heard the doors of the van slam shut and it roared away. Mrs Kindheart ran back to the cottage to telephone the police.

She informed Mister Inspector that Katie had been taken.

Meanwhile Mister Savage drove furiously towards the city. Katie, who was in the rear of the van, couldn't see where they were going because the windows were painted black. But she knew from the sound of the traffic that they were entering the city.

When the van stopped Mister Savage opened the doors and she was allowed out. She found herself in a high-walled courtyard which could only be entered by strong steel doors. Mister Savage had already closed and bolted them and there was no way to escape.

In the courtyard stood a dark forbidding building. The brickwork was slimy and crumbling away. Most of the windows were broken. Dirty curtains flapped in the evening breeze. One tall chimney belched thick black smoke into the darkening sky. But despite her fear, Katie knew where she was. This was The Thieves' Den, the headquarters of Mister Carbuncle.

As she stared around, Mister Savage grabbed her again and dragged her into the building. Once inside he flung her into a room and there to greet her was Mister Illegal.

'Welcome to The Thieves' Den,' Mister Illegal chortled. 'We're delighted to have you here.'

'What do you want with me?' Katie demanded in a firm

voice, pretending she wasn't scared. But she was trembling like a leaf in the wind.

'We'd like you to stay with us for a little while,' Mister Illegal laughed. 'Until Mister Carbuncle and his gang are released from prison, to be exact.'

'They'll never be released,' Katie said, just as firmly.

At this Mister Savage growled deep in his throat and Katie stepped away from him. Mister Illegal laughed again.

'I think they will be released,' he said. 'If they're not, we'll take the steel pins out of your left leg. If that doesn't bring their release we'll take the pins out of your right leg. Then you won't be able to walk again. I think Mister Mayor will release Mister Carbuncle and his gang rather than allow that to happen. You see, the people love you – why I don't know. But they do and they would never elect Mister Mayor again if he let anything happen to you. So the threat of removing the pins should ensure we get what we want.'

'Can I remove the pins?' Mister Savage asked. 'I'd love to.' With that he took his pincers from his pocket and began to open and close it.

'In good time,' Mister Illegal said. 'All in good time. Now take her down to the cellar and lock her up. Tomorrow we'll take her to that Haggard woman I told you about last time. She'll guard her well.'

Mister Savage laughed and grabbed Katie by the arm. He dragged her down to the cellar, to the very room where Mister Carbuncle once kept his chests of gold and jewels. Here Mister Savage threw her into the room and locked the steel door, leaving her all alone in the dark. There Katie cried for Timmy and her foster parents and Friendly Cottage. She cried and cried until she had no tears left.

8
The Kidnappers' Demands

The bus dropped Timmy Goodfellow at City Park. Already the funfair was in full swing and the swirling lights painted streaks of colour against the darkening sky. The screams of children rent the evening air and as Timmy entered he was already growing excited.

He found his friend, Teddy Needy, and they pushed their way through the throngs of people to the bouncing castle. Here the man who operated the castle put Timmy in charge of collecting the money while Teddy was given the job of attending to the equipment which supplied the castle with air. Then the man went off for his tea.

Both boys were kept very busy and were well rewarded when the man returned.

'You've done a good job,' he told them as he paid their wage. 'Tomorrow you can change places, Timmy. Teddy here will show you how to operate the compressor which supplies the air.'

'Thanks,' Timmy answered, delighted. Operating the compressor would be much more fun than collecting money.

Teddy showed Timmy how to operate the compressor straightaway.

'These two valves,' he explained, 'control the supply of air and a special gas. The gas gives the castle extra bounce. You must always ensure the needle on this dial here never enters the area marked in red.'

'That seems easy,' Timmy said.

'Of course it is,' Teddy laughed. 'Now we must go and relieve the boy helping with the waltzers. He'll want his tea too.'

At the waltzers they were given the job of watching the speed control. They sat and watched the dial, both tense with concentration. If the waltzers went too fast it could cause a serious accident.

When the boy returned the man in charge offered them a free ride. Soon they were being whirled around at speed. They shot towards the barriers and the crowd, and when it seemed as if they would fly out into the night, their capsule swung away and headed for the opposite barrier. On and on and around they swung, the waltzer gaining speed until the world outside was a blur.

They couldn't help but scream and their screams mingled with the screams of the other children, who were experiencing the same death-defying sensations. When the ride stopped the two boys were exhausted and had to rest before moving on.

They were helping with the Skyrocket when suddenly the blaring music stopped. The suddenness stilled them and as a last child's scream died away, the silence became intense. Timmy stared at Teddy in puzzlement. Nothing like this had ever happened before.

'Attention! Attention!' A disembodied voice came over the loudspeakers. 'Would Timmy Goodfellow please come to the manager's office immediately? I repeat, immediately.' Even over the loudspeakers Timmy could sense the urgency in the voice.

'Go on, Timmy,' Teddy urged. 'I can manage here.'

Certain that something terrible had happened, Timmy pushed his way through the crowds to the manager's office. Even as he approached he could see the police cars outside. Sick with fear he entered the office to find Mister Inspector waiting for him.

'I'm afraid I've got bad news, Timmy,' Mister Inspector

said. His face was grave and his right cheek twitched. 'Katie has been taken.'

'Oh, no!' It was all Timmy could say. His face grew pale and he began to tremble. It took an enormous effort to speak again. 'Who ... who did it?' he asked. 'And why? Why Katie?'

'We don't know yet,' Mister Inspector said. 'But no doubt someone will demand a ransom for her.'

'Mister Carbuncle.' Timmy spoke slowly and carefully.

'He's still in prison,' Mister Inspector said. 'We checked immediately we learned what had happened. He was safely locked up in his cell.'

'He has something to do with it.' Timmy spoke with certainty. 'We should go and search The Thieves' Den immediately.'

'I'm afraid we can't,' Mister Inspector said. 'Mister Illegal knows the law. We'd need a warrant and no judge will give us one without good cause. I'm afraid there's nothing we can do until we get a demand from whoever's taken her.'

Timmy was still convinced Mister Carbuncle was responsible. And if the police couldn't act then he'd have to act himself. But first he must go home to his foster parents. They'd be terribly worried that something might have happened to him too.

'Could you take me home, please?' Timmy asked, and

Mister Inspector ordered one of his men to do so.

The journey seemed interminable and as soon as the car pulled into the drive of Friendly Cottage Timmy leapt out. His foster parents were waiting at the door and Mrs Kindheart sobbed with relief when she saw he was safe.

'This is terrible, Timmy,' she sobbed. 'Poor Katie. She'll be so frightened. I keep thinking we'll never see her again.'

'Of course we'll see her,' Timmy reassured her, bravely, desperately trying to hide his doubts. His heart was breaking but he knew he had to be brave. Katie might have to depend on him to save her.

'Timmy's right,' Mister Kindheart said. 'Katie'll be fine.' He spoke firmly but Timmy caught a glimpse of moisture in his eyes. Mister Kindheart loved Katie very much. If anything happened to her he'd be heartbroken. So many people's happiness depended on him, Timmy realised, and he shivered at the thought of the responsibility.

They entered the cottage and Timmy saw Mister Policeman sitting by the telephone in the hall. He was waiting for a call from the kidnappers. As Timmy passed the sitting room door he heard someone go: 'Pssstt.'

He turned and saw Mister Tom beckoning him with a paw.

'I saw the man who took Katie,' Mister Tom miaowed.

'He was the ugliest man I've ever seen in my life. His face was twisted and covered with spots of dried blood.'

'Mister Savage.' Timmy whispered the name. 'I saw his picture and read about him when Mr Carbuncle was sent to prison. It was him I saw earlier today. He doesn't shave but pulls out the hair with a pincers. That's what causes all those spots.'

'He looked terribly cruel,' Mister Tom said. 'You must try and rescue Katie from him. The cottage just wouldn't be the same without her.' Mister Tom's voice broke and his tail quivered.

'I read that Mister Savage once worked for Mister Carbuncle,' Timmy said. 'I know he's behind all this. He's taken Katie to have revenge on me. Now I must ...' But Timmy got no further, for just then the telephone rang.

Mister and Mrs Kindheart rushed from the kitchen. They all gathered around the telephone while Mister Policeman took notes. No one dared breathe as Mister Policeman finished writing in his notebook and hung up the receiver.

'That was a demand from the kidnappers,' he said.

'What do they want?' Mister Kindheart demanded. 'How much money are they asking for?'

'They don't want money,' Mister Policeman said quietly.

'Don't want money,' Mister Kindheart repeated. 'So what do they want?'

'I'm so sorry,' Mister Policeman said. 'But they've threatened to take the steel pins out of Katie's legs so she won't be able to walk again.' He shook his head and dabbed his eyes with the sleeve of his uniform.

'Unless we do what?' Mister Kindheart demanded. 'What do they want from us?'

'They want Mister Carbuncle and his thugs released from prison,' Mister Policeman whispered. 'That's what they want.'

'Oh no!' Mrs Kindheart whimpered and swayed. Her husband caught her and led her back to the kitchen. Mister Tom and Timmy exchanged glances. Timmy swallowed hard and bit his lower lip, clenching his fists.

'It's up to you now, Timmy,' Mister Tom said, quietly. 'If anyone can save Katie, you can.'

9
A Shock for Katie

Timmy realised Mister Tom could be speaking the truth. Katie's safety might be in his hands. Right now she was probably at The Thieves' Den, maybe tied up in the cellar where he himself had once been a prisoner.

Timmy shivered at the memory of that terrible time when he had been a prisoner of Mister Carbuncle's. But his friends, the rats and mice, had come to his rescue. Now he must come to Katie's rescue. There was no time to lose.

Without thought for his own safety, Timmy slipped out of the cottage. It was dark outside and cold, and he turned up the collar of his jacket. He ran down the drive and as he reached the gates he heard the scream of a police siren. He ducked close to the hedge as the car turned into the drive and he had a glimpse of Mister Inspector as it sped past.

Timmy stepped out of his hiding place just as Mister Reporter arrived in his television van. Timmy didn't have a chance to hide again and he was spotted. The van stopped and Mister Reporter leapt out, thrusting a microphone under Timmy's nose.

'The news has just broken,' Mister Reporter said. 'We've heard that Katie's kidnappers are demanding the release of Mister Carbuncle and his gang. Is this correct Timmy?'

Timmy nodded. He couldn't really speak.

'Do you know where Katie is being held?' Mister Reporter asked.

'I think she might be ... anywhere,' Timmy mumbled. He'd been about to say he was convinced she was being held at The Thieves' Den. But he didn't want to warn the kidnappers of his suspicions.

'I see,' Mister Reporter said. He now turned and faced the camera. 'This is Mister Reporter,' he said, 'live from Friendly Cottage. I'm now handing you back to the studio.'

With that he leaped back into the van which raced up the driveway in the wake of the police car. Timmy watched the red lights for a moment and then turned his face towards the city and The Thieves' Den.

'Didn't he look scared?' Mister Savage threw up his hands and laughed. 'And they say he's brave! Why, he was trembling with fear.' Mister Savage laughed again and looked maliciously at Mister Illegal.

They were sitting in the operations' room at The Thieves' Den, watching the television for developments. While Mister Savage laughed the lawyer was frowning. He had watched the interview carefully and noticed the hesitation when Timmy was questioned as to Katie's whereabouts. Mister Illegal was convinced Timmy had been about to tell Mister Reporter where he thought Katie was being held. But he had changed his mind. Why was that? The lawyer pursed his thin lips and the truth dawned on him.

He leapt from his chair and switched off the television.

'Come on,' he said to Mister Savage. 'We must get the girl out of here immediately.'

'Are you mad?' Mister Savage demanded. 'I'm not going anywhere. My favourite cartoons are on now. I think they're brilliant. I love it when everyone gets squashed by falling rocks and run over by trucks. Don't you?'

'No, I don't,' Mister Illegal said. 'Now, we've got to move the girl. That brother of hers knows she's here. We must move her before he comes to rescue her.'

'I'm not scared of him,' Mister Savage said.

'He'll inform the police she's here,' Mister Illegal said. 'If they find her here, then we'll both go to prison. Do you want that?'

'No.' It was Mister Savage's turn to be scared. He hated prison. He hated being locked up and above all he hated having to eat salty lumpy porridge. It made him belch all the time.

'Bring her up from the cellar,' Mister Illegal ordered, 'and put her in the van. We'll take her to Mrs Haggard. Let's hope we're not too late.'

The thought of going to prison made Mister Savage hurry. He ran down to the cellar, to the secret room. Katie had earlier laid down on a thin mattress on the floor and had pulled a threadbare blanket over her. She was dozing, her eyes red and sore from weeping.

Mister Savage grabbed her by the arm and pulled her to her feet. She didn't have a chance to protest as she was dragged upstairs and out to the van. She was thrown into the back of it and the doors were locked.

Mister Savage sat in the driver's seat and soon Mister Illegal came to join him. The lawyer gave directions and Mister Savage followed the route. This brought them to the oldest part of the city. They wound their way through dark, narrow streets where factories belched smoke into the sky from tall finger-like chimneys. Large areas were fenced off with corrugated iron. The houses were dilapidated and rusting cars stood in the streets. The gutters were strewn with litter.

Mister Illegal ordered Mister Savage to stop and he drew up outside the most dilapidated house they had seen so far. The windows were broken and patched with plywood. The front door hung crookedly and there were holes in the roof where slates had been blown off in the storms.

They got out of the van and Mister Illegal walked up the rutted path to the front door. He rapped on the wood and the door opened with a long drawn out squeal. Meanwhile Mister Savage ordered Katie to get out but she cringed away from him. Mister Savage had to climb up into the van to get her. He was angry and grabbed her by the hair, dragging her out onto the roadway. He then caught her arm and propelled her up the path into the house.

It was dark in the hall but despite this Mister Savage could see the woman who stood beside Mister Illegal. He thought she was as ugly and as savage as himself, and the cruel gleam in her eyes frightened him.

'This is Mrs Haggard,' Mister Illegal said. 'She was Katie and Timmy's foster mother once. But Mister Mayor ordered they be taken from her and sent to live with Mister and

Mrs Kindheart. He claimed that Mrs Haggard was cruel. I think myself ...'

But he got no further, for it was then that Katie screamed, a blood-curdling scream that would have made Mister Savage's hair stand on end, if he had any.

'She's obviously pleased to see you, Mrs Haggard,' Mister Illegal laughed.

'Good evening, Miss Katie,' Mrs Haggard hissed. 'How nice of you to call.'

Katie screamed again and again. Indeed she might have kept on screaming if Mrs Haggard hadn't struck her hard across the face.

'Bring her upstairs,' she ordered. 'Let's see if we can teach her manners.'

Mister Savage dragged Katie up to the attic.

'I'll let her have her old room back,' Mrs Haggard said. 'She'll feel at home then.'

Mister Savage threw Katie into the room. It was bare except for a narrow iron bed. The window was boarded up and there were holes in the roof. The bed and floor were wet from the rain and the walls were covered with thick green slime.

'I'll get some planks and a hammer and nails,' Mrs Haggard said. 'The door has rotted away so you'll need to block up the opening. We don't want the nice little girl running away before we take the pins out of her legs.'

Mrs Haggard left the room and Katie grabbed Mister Savage's sleeve.

'Don't leave me here,' she begged. 'Please take me back to the cellar. I'll lie on the stone floor and I won't even use the blanket. I won't be any trouble. I won't even cry when you take the pins out of my legs.'

Mister Savage turned away. He was known to be one of the cruellest men in The Underworld. No one would ever willingly wish to be his prisoner. Yet this girl would prefer to be with him than with Mrs Haggard. Clearly he had now met someone who was even more cruel than himself. He wanted to do as the girl asked. He wanted to take her back to the cellar. But he had a job to do. He couldn't let his feelings come into it.

Mrs Haggard returned. While Katie pleaded for mercy, Mister Savage nailed the planks across the opening. Then he went downstairs, his hands clapped over his ears to drown out the prisoner's cries for mercy.

10
At the Thieves' Den

When Timmy Goodfellow reached The Thieves' Den he crouched down by the high wall which surrounded it. There was no street lighting here and the area was dark and dismal. Cloud had blotted out the moon and an oppressive silence hung above the streets.

Timmy knew he was in grave danger. If he were caught inside the fortress he would be taken prisoner like Katie. But he had to face the danger. He had to try and rescue her.

The high wall surrounding The Thieves' Den was built of brick and was topped with barbed wire. The brick was old and crumbling away, and gave good hand and footholds which Timmy now used to climb upwards. He made good progress, hanging on at times by his toes and the tips of his fingers.

He was near the top when disaster nearly struck. A piece of brick crumbled away and his foot slipped. As he struggled desperately to hang on, his other foot also slipped from its precarious hold. Timmy found himself hanging on by his fingernails high above the pavement.

Had he panicked he would have fallen. But Timmy kept his head and sought a foothold with his toes. Just when he was certain he would fall, he located a foothold and was able to take a rest. But urgency drove him on and he climbed to the top of the wall. Here strands of barbed wire were strung along the wall. But the gap between the bottom strand and the wall was just large enough for a boy of Timmy's size to slip underneath.

Timmy did so and climbed down into the courtyard. He ran across the cobbled yard and crouched by the rear of the building. Beside him there was a window without glass. A piece of cardboard blocked up the opening. Timmy tore away the cardboard and clambered into The Thieves' Den.

It was pitch black in the room and, with outstretched arms, Timmy moved about until he found the door. He opened it carefully but still the unoiled hinges creaked. He held his breath, waiting for someone to pounce on him. But nothing happened.

Timmy now found himself in a narrow passageway. He

was becoming accustomed to the gloom and he could see that the passageway was long. Doors opened off it on both sides. Timmy looked in each room in turn. They were damp and musty and, though he whispered Katie's name, there was no answer.

He searched the ground floor and then went down to the cellar. In the room where he had once been a prisoner, he shivered at the memory. But he plucked up courage and continued his search. It proved fruitless. Katie wasn't here.

As he came back up from the cellar he heard a vehicle enter the courtyard. Doors slammed and footsteps approached the rear door. Realising the danger he was in, Timmy ducked into one of the rooms, leaving the door slightly ajar.

He heard voices as two men entered the passageway. A light was switched on and he peered out. He saw Mister Illegal and another man. This man had his back to Timmy and when he turned around, it took all Timmy's courage not to cry out, for he found himself looking at the ugly face of Mister Savage.

'What do we do now?' Mister Savage asked in his high-pitched voice.

'Nothing,' Mister Illegal answered. 'The girl is safe. The police will never find her. Nor will that brother of hers.

He's dangerous and we'll have to watch out for him.'

'I could deal with him,' Mister Savage said. 'I could break his arms and legs if you like.'

'Better not,' Mister Illegal warned. 'Mister Carbuncle will want to do that himself.'

'Do you think he'll get out of prison?' Mister Savage asked.

'Of course,' the lawyer replied. 'Mister Carbuncle will be a free man tomorrow. Now I'll ...'

But just then they heard the sound of police sirens. Cars raced to a stop outside with screeching brakes and tyres.

'It's the police,' Mister Savage whimpered like a baby. 'We're ruined. I'll be put in prison. I'll ...'

'Shut up!' Mister Illegal grabbed the thug's arm. 'They can't touch us,' he hissed. 'They have no evidence. Just keep your mouth shut and let me do the talking.'

Outside there was a tremendous banging as the police broke down the doors to the courtyard. Then a large group of burly policemen, led my Mister Inspector, burst into the passageway.

'Search the place,' Mister Inspector ordered. 'Make sure you don't miss any nook or cranny.'

The policemen spread out, leaving Mister Inspector in the hallway with Mister Illegal and Mister Savage.

'You've no right to do this,' Mister Illegal said in his lawyer's voice. 'I know the law.'

'We've got a search warrant,' Mister Inspector answered. He waved a piece of paper under Mister Illegal's nose.

'Maybe if you told me who you're looking for,' Mister Illegal suggested, 'I might be able to help you.'

'You know well who we're looking for,' Mister Inspector said angrily. 'And we'll find her without your help.'

'I don't know what you're talking about,' Mister Illegal said. 'Do you know, Mister Savage?'

Mister Savage opened his mouth to speak. But before he could utter a word, Timmy Goodfellow could stand it no longer. He rushed from his hiding place, taking everyone by surprise.

'He's lying,' Timmy cried out. 'Mister Savage kidnapped Katie. They've hidden her somewhere. I just heard them talking about it.'

'Katie?' Mister Illegal said. 'I did hear that name before.' He scratched his head. 'Now, where did I hear it?'

'Don't pretend you don't know,' Timmy said. 'You know Katie is my sister. You've kidnapped her and threatened to take the steel pins out of her legs so she won't be able to walk again. You'll do that if Mister Carbuncle isn't released from prison.'

'She's been kidnapped, has she?' Mister Illegal asked.

'Well, serves her right. She's a horrid child. I hope she's being held in a dark damp cellar somewhere. Did you know that dampness causes rust? The pins in her legs will go rusty. That'll make her suffer.'

Timmy couldn't take any more. He rushed at Mister Illegal with clenched fists but Mister Inspector grabbed his shoulder.

'Arrest him for assault,' Mister Illegal said. 'And for breaking and entering. I know the law. I have rights. I ...'

'Shut up,' Mister Inspector ordered, in a cold voice. 'Or I'll arrest you for obstructing the law. Now, I'll ask you again. Is Katie Goodfellow here in this house?'

'Of course not,' Mister Illegal said. 'I wouldn't have that horrid child here. Now, if you don't mind, I have business to attend to.' With that he strode away, followed by Mister Savage.

'Arrest them,' Timmy pleaded. 'They have kidnapped Katie. Mister Savage did it. They've hidden her somewhere in the city.'

'I know they have,' Mister Inspector said. 'But I have no evidence against them. I'm afraid I can't arrest them Timmy. But let me assure you we're doing everything we can to find Katie. Every policeman and woman in the city is looking for her. When they heard she'd been kidnapped they volunteered to help in the search.'

Timmy was moved by the news. Katie was loved by everyone. But that wouldn't be much good if they couldn't find her. If the steel pins were removed and she couldn't walk again, Timmy knew his heart would break.

'Keep your spirits up, Timmy,' Mister Inspector said. 'We may still find some evidence here.'

But the search proved fruitless. There was no sign that Katie had ever been here. Mister Inspector looked perturbed and the policemen stood about in the hall not talking, their eyes downcast on the floor.

'What now?' Timmy asked.

Mister Inspector shook his head.

'We must report to Mister Mayor,' he said. 'He's personally taken charge of the case. He must decide whether to give in to the kidnappers' demands and release Mister Carbuncle and his gang. Come with me, Timmy. We'll go and see Mister Mayor right away.'

11
Mister Mayor's Decision

That evening Mister Mayor was a worried man. An election was due to be held in a month and he knew that if anything happened to Katie Goodfellow the people would not vote for him. But he also realised that Mister Carbuncle was the most hated man in the city. If he released him, that too might upset the people who had suffered for so long at his hands.

Nervously Mister Mayor fingered his chain of office. It was made of gold and was encrusted with jewels. Mister Mayor loved to wear it around his neck. If he weren't re-elected then he would never get to wear the chain again. And he wouldn't have his limousine or his big dinners or his champagne. And Madam Mayor would never forgive him. She loved the pomp and ceremony and having everyone curtseying to her.

If she lost that she'd make her husband's life a misery.

'Well,' Mister Mayor said now, turning to his advisor. 'What do you suggest I do?'

Mister Advisor scratched his nose. Then he scratched his ear. Then he licked his lips and scratched his nose again. 'I think, Mister Mayor,' he said very slowly, 'that you should release Mister Carbuncle, for if anything terrible should happen to Katie Goodfellow the people of the city will never forgive you.'

'I see,' Mister Mayor said, nodding. 'And what happens when Mister Carbuncle starts to terrorise the citizens? What then?'

Mister Advisor scratched his nose. Then he scratched his ear. As his tongue popped out to lick his lips, Mister Mayor erupted like a volcano.

'Answer the question,' he shouted. 'Stop scratching yourself like a cat with fleas.'

'I ...' Mister Advisor began, his hand automatically going to his nose. It stopped short, however, and Mister Advisor tried to begin again. But before he could speak they both heard the sound of police sirens.

The two men waited in silence and then heard footsteps on the marble floor outside. The massive oak doors to the chamber were flung open and Mister Inspector entered, followed by Timmy Goodfellow. Mister Mayor jumped to his feet, anxious for news.

'We haven't found Katie Goodfellow,' Mister Inspector began. 'I've had The Thieves' Den searched from top to bottom but there's no sign of her. Mister Illegal has hidden her somewhere in the city. But we'll continue searching for her.'

'The deadline is tomorrow,' Mister Mayor said. 'If Mister Carbuncle isn't released by then, the pins will be removed from one of Katie's legs. Can you find her before that?'

'It's unlikely,' Mister Inspector said. 'This is a big city. They could have hidden her anywhere.'

'You must release Mister Carbuncle, Mister Mayor,' Timmy pleaded. 'You can't allow them to hurt Katie. Please, sir, you must.'

Mister Mayor sighed. This was the most difficult decision he had ever had to make. He turned to Mister Advisor and opened his mouth to speak. But Mister Advisor's hand flew to his nose.

'I haven't even asked a question,' Mister Mayor shouted in exasperation, and Mister Inspector and Timmy Goodfellow stared at him in amazement.

It was now Mister Mayor's turn to scratch his head. He also scratched his nose and bit his lower lip. Then, quite suddenly, he came to attention.

'I've made my decision,' he said. 'I'm going to release Mister Carbuncle tomorrow at noon. That way Katie will be safe. Now, have my limousine brought around immediately,' he added to Mister Advisor. 'I must go home and rest. These decisions drain my strength.'

'Thank you Mister Mayor,' Timmy said. 'When I speak to Mister Reporter I'll tell him you did the right thing and that everyone should vote for you.'

'Thank you, Timmy,' Mister Mayor said. He was feeling better already. If Timmy Goodfellow, the most popular boy in the city, advised people to vote for Mister Mayor, they would certainly do so. He would be re-elected and get to keep his chain and limousine.

Mister Mayor felt relieved. He strode out of his chambers, his mayoral robes flowing behind him. Mister Advisor scuttled after him and in his haste stood on the hem of the robe. He tripped and fell on his face and Timmy Goodfellow couldn't help but smile. It was the first time he had even smiled since Katie had been kidnapped.

'I suppose I'd best take you home,' Mister Inspector said. 'Tomorrow Katie will be home again, safe and well.'

That night Timmy could hardly sleep. He tossed and turned in his soft bed and thought of Katie. Was she OK? Did she have a soft warm bed of her own? Or was she hungry and frightened? Timmy felt tears in his eyes and he wiped them away with the back of his hand.

Earlier he had watched Mister Reporter announce on television that Mister Carbuncle would be released the next day at noon. At six that evening Katie Goodfellow would be released. The kidnappers had given their word on that. Timmy knew he should have been delighted with the news. But he only felt apprehensive. He knew something could still go wrong.

He closed his eyes and tried to sleep. But a scratching noise at the window disturbed him. He listened and the noise came again.

'Katie?' He spoke the word aloud as he leapt from the bed and rushed to the window. He didn't even stop to think that his room was in the attic and that Katie couldn't have reached the window. Still hopeful that it was Katie, he drew the curtains and peered out into the darkness. But all he saw was his own reflection.

'I only imagined it,' he thought and turned to go back to bed.

'Timmy. Timmy.' A weak voice called his name insistently from outside the window.

Timmy swung back and threw the window open wide. Sitting on the windowsill, looking up at him, were Mousey Mouse and Ratty Rat.

'Thought you'd never open up,' Ratty complained, gruffly.

'It's quite understandable,' Mousey said in a conciliatory tone of voice. 'He has a lot on his mind.'

'That's why we're here,' Ratty said. He still spoke gruffly but Timmy knew he didn't mean it. Ratty was old and suffered from arthritis, which caused him a lot of pain. 'We've heard about Katie,' Ratty went on. 'So we've come to offer our help. I can have 5,000 rats scouring the city for Katie within minutes of my giving the orders.'

'And I can have 10,000 mice,' Mousey added. 'Just say the word Timmy, and the search can begin.'

Timmy hadn't thought of his friends. He should have turned to them for assistance. The birds would have helped too, because Timmy and Katie always made sure they were fed. Even when the children lived with Mrs Haggard they had shared what little food they got with the birds, and with Ratty and Mousey too.

'Well ...' Timmy murmured. 'Well I never ... I ...'

'Stop mumbling,' Ratty ordered, 'and make up your mind. That fine sister of yours is out there somewhere right now. She's probably cold and hungry and frightened and ...' Ratty's voice broke and he coughed, placing a paw to his mouth. 'Look,' he said, even more gruffly than usual, 'do you want us to search for her or not? Come on. Speak up.'

'Please,' Timmy managed to say. 'Please search for her. If

anyone can find her, you can.'

'We can try, Timmy,' Mousey said. 'But we can't promise anything. It's a big city and there's not a lot of time left. I just heard that Mister Carbuncle is to be released at noon. But we'll do our best. You can ...'

'Will you stop blathering, Mousey,' Ratty said. 'And let us get on with it. I've never known anyone talk so much.'

'Sorry, Ratty,' Mousey apologised. 'I'm ready.'

'About time too,' Ratty said. 'Well, we'll be seeing you, Timmy.' With that he scurried onto the thatched roof. Mousey winked at Timmy and followed his friend into the darkness.

Timmy closed the window and returned to bed. He felt more relaxed now. Ratty and Mousey knew every nook and cranny in the city and would surely find Katie. Timmy eventually slept and dreamed of Katie. They were together again, playing in the garden as they used to.

But as Timmy was dreaming, Katie lay awake on the wet mattress in her old room at Mrs Haggard's house. She was tired, cold and hungry. Mrs Haggard had refused her food or blankets and had threatened to beat her if she made any noise.

Katie knew Mrs Haggard wanted her to plead for mercy. But Katie Goodfellow would never plead. She set her face to the wall and huddled up for warmth as the cold draughts whirled about her. It was going to be a very long night.

12
Carbuncle Goes Free

*A*ll through the night the mice and rats searched the city. Whiskers and Junior Rat had been instructed to search the street where Mrs Haggard lived. But when they came to the house, they hesitated.

'Ratty warned us never to enter this place,' Junior whispered. 'Not under any circumstances, he said.'

'We'd best not go in then,' Whiskers said, and they slipped by and searched the remaining houses. When they had completed the search they returned to report to Ratty. But they didn't mention that they hadn't searched Mrs Haggard's house.

Through the long night the other rats and mice returned to report their failure to find Katie. At dawn Ratty and Mousey called off the search. It would be much too dangerous to continue during daylight hours. With heavy hearts, Mousey and Ratty made their way to Friendly Cottage to report to Timmy.

Timmy thanked them for their help.

'You've done a good job,' he said. 'You can't be blamed for not finding Katie. Now we must wait until Mister Carbuncle is released. I'm going to the prison myself to see it.'

At noon Timmy was outside the city prison. A large crowd had gathered to await this terrible event. The crowd were in an ugly mood and big policemen struggled to keep them behind the barriers.

At precisely twelve o'clock the massive gates to the prison swung open and Mister Carbuncle swaggered out. Timmy hardly recognised him. He had lost so much weight! His face though looked more evil than ever. He was followed by Mister Vicious and the other thugs.

The crowd hissed and booed, and Mister Carbuncle shook his fists at them. The other thugs copied their Boss as they followed him to the limousine that was waiting. Mister Savage was driving while Mister Illegal sat beside him. Once the thugs were safely in the car it sped off.

The television van covering the release followed the crooks. Mister Reporter spotted Timmy and ordered the driver to stop.

'Come with us, Timmy,' Mister Reporter said. 'I want to get your reactions to all this.'

They caught up with the limousine and kept it in sight as it sped through the city. In the limousine Mister Carbuncle was beginning to relax and enjoy himself. He had begun to fear this day would never come. He could hardly believe he was free, and he stared excitedly from the window.

'There's a post office, Boss,' Mister Vicious pointed out. 'Maybe we could stop and rob it?'

'Are you stupid?' Mister Carbuncle glared. 'Can't you see the television crew are right behind us.'

'Sorry, Boss,' Mister Vicious said humbly. 'I didn't think.'

'It's lucky you've got me to think for you,' Mister Carbuncle said. He continued staring from the window and up ahead he spotted a giant plastic cone on the pavement. It was advertising ice-cream. 'Stop the car,' he ordered. 'I want ice-cream. Go and get me some.'

As the limousine stopped each of the thugs tried to do as their Boss said. They climbed all over each other as they struggled to get out of the car. One lost his shoe and found himself upside down. His smelly sock ended up beneath Mister Carbuncle's nose and the Boss of The Underworld had to pinch his nostrils.

Eventually Mister Vicious fought his way out of the car. He ran to the shop where a terrified assistant filled a cone with ice-cream. Mister Vicious grabbed it and triumphantly bore it back to the limousine. But his triumph was short lived.

'That?' Mister Carbuncle spluttered. 'I'll eat that in one bite.' He grabbed the cone and did just that. 'Go and get me a large cone,' he ordered. 'And put chocolate sauce on it this time.'

Mister Vicious ran back to the shop. But the terrified assistant had no large cones. Mister Vicious swung around in panic. Just then he spotted the plastic cone on the pavement. He dashed out and grabbed the cone. It had a round pink top and this he unscrewed. Re-entering the shop he gave the cone to the assistant and ordered her to fill it with ice-cream. When the cone was filled Mister Vicious grabbed the bottle of chocolate sauce and poured all of it over the ice-cream. More triumphant than before he bore the giant cone out to the limousine.

But it wouldn't fit inside and Mister Carbuncle stuck his head out the window. While Mister Vicious held the cone, Mister Carbuncle first licked up all the chocolate sauce, which dribbled down the outside of the cone. Then he gulped down the ice-cream piled up on top. Unfortunately Mister Vicious had forgotten to warn his Boss that the cone was made of plastic and it was this that caused the disaster.

Mister Carbuncle was the greediest man in the world. He couldn't get at the ice-cream in the cone quickly enough. So he opened his mouth wide and took a great big bite. Or at least he tried to do so. But his teeth couldn't bite through the tough plastic. Instead they broke in his mouth and he bellowed with pain and rage. He caught Mister Vicious by the throat and tried to drag him through the limousine window.

As the two men struggled, Mister Carbuncle lashed out wildly with his feet. He kicked the thugs who were with him in the limousine and, as they tried to avoid his flailing feet, one of them struck the switch which operated the electric window. The window closed, trapping Mister Carbuncle's head and hands. He was forced to release his grip and when he did so, Mister Vicious dropped the cone and ran away.

Just then Teddy Needy came along the street on his way to the funfair. He saw what had happened and, aware of the pain Mister Carbuncle had caused Timmy Goodfellow, Teddy decided to wreak some vengeance on the Boss of The Underworld.

He ran over and picked up the cone. It was still full of

ice-cream, which had begun to melt. Teddy held the cone over the trapped thug and poured the contents on top of his head. When the cone was empty, Teddy gave Mister Carbuncle a dozen sharp blows about the ears before he too dropped the cone and ran to safety.

The ice-cream poured down Mister Carbuncle's neck. It was cold and tickly. It ran into his ears and when he tried to raise his head, the sticky mess ran into his eyes, blinding him. He was still struggling to escape while in the limousine the thugs were desperately trying to keep out of reach of his flailing steel-capped boots.

It was Mister Illegal who came to the rescue. In the front seat, safe from the steel-capped kicks, he reached the switch which operated the rear electric window. He pressed the switch and as the window opened, one of the thugs dragged Mister Carbuncle back inside.

As the limousine sped on the television crew followed it. Mister Cameraman had filmed everything and Timmy Goodfellow realised it was the very thing to cheer Katie when she was released later that day.

13
Treachery

Poor Katie had hardly slept the previous night. Some time near dawn she did nod off and later awoke cold and hungry. She struggled to her feet and walked to the window to look out through a chink in the plywood. She saw the rundown houses and the sooty factories, a familiar sight from the days when she and Timmy lived here with Mrs Haggard after their parents were killed in the road accident. Katie had lived in this room, a virtual prisoner, unable to walk as a result of the accident. Then Timmy had rescued Santa Claus from Mister Carbuncle who had tried to take over Christmas. As a reward for saving Christmas Mister Mayor had taken herself and Timmy away from here to live in Friendly Cottage.

Katie had thought then that she would never see this

house or Mrs Haggard again. But here she was now, a prisoner once more. And if Mister Carbuncle didn't get his way, she would end up crippled once again when the pins were removed from her legs.

Katie shivered and bit her lip. She didn't want to cry but tears welled up in her eyes and she wiped them away. She stared from the window, wondering how she might escape. Just then she heard footsteps on the stairs. She turned to see Mrs Haggard push her breakfast between the planks blocking the doorway.

'Look what I've found,' Mrs Haggard said, taking something from the pocket of her dirty greasy apron.

Katie stared as Mrs Haggard held up a pliers. They were a foot long and were coated with rust. Mrs Haggard opened and closed the pliers and the gaping jaws resembled the mouth of a prehistoric animal.

'Just look,' Mrs Haggard gloated. 'They'll pull the pins out.' She opened and closed the pliers once more and Katie felt sick. Katie turned away but this only made Mrs Haggard laugh. It was a horrible cackling sound like someone scraping nails on a blackboard.

When Mrs Haggard went away Katie checked her breakfast. There was a crust of stale bread and a dirty cup, half filled with water. Katie retched and knew she couldn't eat or drink anything. But she could still feed the birds as she did every morning, though she was sad she didn't have bird-seed for them. They would still like the stale bread though.

She broke the bread into crumbs. These she pushed through the chink in the plywood and they fell onto the windowsill. Then Katie walked back to the bed and threw herself down on it, the image of the gaping jaws of the pliers still vivid in her mind.

When Mister Carbuncle reached The Thieves' Den he ordered his thugs to bring him ice-cream. They went out into the city and stole an ice-cream van which they brought back to the courtyard. There the operator was forced to supply Mister Carbuncle with large bowls of ice-cream topped with chocolate, strawberry and raspberry sauce.

Mister Carbuncle sat in his leather chair in the operations' room and ate the ice-cream with a soup ladle. Mister Illegal hovered nearby like a starved crow and anxiously watched. He had hidden his wig in case Mister Carbuncle went back on his word and made him eat it.

'Well,' Mister Carbuncle demanded, 'what's this plan you've got to make me rich?'

'Let me show you a video first,' Mister Illegal said. 'Then I'll explain everything.'

With that he scurried over to the television and switched it on. Then he pressed the button marked Play on the video recorder. The recording was of Timmy and Katie Goodfellow's appearance on The Latest Latest Show.

'What's this?' Mister Carbuncle demanded. 'I don't want to see them. They put me off my ice-cream.'

Mister Illegal cringed and bowed.

'Please watch it,' he pleaded. 'Then I'll explain my plan to make you the richest man in the world. And,' he went on triumphantly, 'it will also destroy Toyland and Santa Claus.'

Mister Carbuncle's eyes popped. His mouth hung open and ice-cream and red sauce dribbled down his chin. He stared at the television, his heart beating wildly. He listened now as Timmy explained all about the ozone layer and how it was causing the ice to melt. Mister Carbuncle dropped the soup ladle and clapped his hands with delight.

But his delight was short-lived for when the show ended it was announced that governments were to take immediate action to prevent further pollution. Mister Carbuncle's face became enflamed and his breath came out like puffs of black smoke.

'How dare you show me such nonsense,' he screamed. 'Get your wig immediately. I'm going to make you eat it right now.'

'Please,' Mister Illegal begged. 'Let me explain. I've got

a plan all worked out. I've filed a claim on the land beneath the ice. The claim is in your name. You'll own the rights to all the gold and the oil. You'll be the richest, most powerful man in the world.'

'But the ice isn't going to melt,' Mister Carbuncle wailed, thinking of all the riches that could be his.

'Oh, but it is,' Mister Illegal said, his courage returning. 'We're going to melt it.'

'Melt it?' Mister Carbuncle roared. 'Melt it? How do you propose to melt it? Set fire to the North Pole? Is that it? Or use that hot air you're spouting? Do we dangle you by the legs over the North Pole and leave you hanging there until the ice melts?'

'Goodness me, no,' Mister Illegal laughed, thinking his Boss had cracked a joke. 'We destroy the ozone layer. Then the sun will melt the ice.'

'Oh I see,' Mister Carbuncle said sarcastically. 'We're going to destroy the ozone layer with your hot air.'

Mister Illegal couldn't stop giggling. His Boss could be so funny sometimes. He held his sides as he laughed. But Mister Carbuncle couldn't see the joke. In a temper he threw the bowl of ice-cream and it struck the lawyer on the head. Mr Illegal cried out in pain as the ice-cream splattered his face and black suit.

'Explain your plan,' Mister Carbuncle threatened. 'And remember, this is your last chance.'

Mister Illegal cleaned the ice-cream from his face.

'My plan is simple,' he said. 'Mister Kindheart owns a factory which makes aerosols. So we get him to make us some giant aerosol cans and fill them with the deadly chemicals that destroy the ozone layer. Then we take the cans to the North Pole and release the chemicals. I've had Mister Brains work out the details. Within a month Toyland will disappear forever.'

Mister Carbuncle sat up in his chair. He was interested now. His eyes were filled with greed and in his mind he could see chests filled with gold and jewels. For a few moments he began to dream. Then reality struck him and anger showed on his face.

'You've forgotten one thing,' he said quietly. 'And for that – for making me suffer like this – I'm going to make you eat all the lawyers' wigs in the whole city. How?' Mister Carbuncle roared suddenly, making Mister Illegal jump in the air. 'How do you propose to make Mister Kindheart co-operate with us? Are we just going to ask him?'

'In a way,' Mister Illegal said.

'And why should he help us?' Mister Carbuncle asked. His voice was laced with deadly menace.

'Because we've got Katie Goodfellow,' Mister Illegal explained quietly. 'While we have her Mister Kindheart will do anything we ask.'

'We don't let her go?' pondered Mister Carbuncle. 'Is that it?'

'Exactly,' Mister Illegal said. 'We keep her a prisoner until we have the aerosol cans at the North Pole. After that no one can stop us.'

'It's ... it's brilliant,' Mister Carbuncle spluttered. 'Brilliant. It's the best plan I've ever had.' He clapped his hands with glee. 'Get me another bowl of ice-cream,' he ordered. 'I want to celebrate. Oh yes, I'm going to be the richest man in the world.'

Mister Carbuncle threw his legs up in the air. But his chair toppled over and he landed heavily on the floor. He hit his head and knocked himself out, and lay there dreaming of untold riches.

14
Tricked by Carbuncle

That very day Salty Seagull decided to visit his friends in the city. He had so much to tell them about his adventures at the seaside. He ate a light breakfast before setting off, because it was difficult to fly on a full stomach. It caused indigestion and wind.

It was a long flight across the open countryside. There was a stiff wind blowing and it drained Salty's energy. By lunchtime he was tired and hungry and decided to have a quick snack and a little rest before completing the journey.

He spotted a farmyard and flew towards it, keeping a wary eye out for danger. But all seemed quiet. As he approached he saw a chicken run and knew from experience that there would be food there.

He landed on a post supporting the wire mesh encircling the run. Immediately the hens began to squawk and a rooster, who had been inside the chicken coop, emerged.

'What do you want?' Rusty Rooster demanded. 'You know you just can't come round here disturbing my girls. It stops them from laying.'

'Sorry,' Salty said. 'But I've just flown from the seaside and I'm hungry.'

'I suppose we can spare some food,' Rusty said. 'But you'd best be quick. Brushy Fox has been about and Mister Farmer is keeping an eye out for him. He'll be coming to check on us soon.'

'I'll be quick,' Salty said. 'And thanks.'

He hopped down into the run and began to peck the grain scattered on the black earth. Rusty and his girls gathered around to watch the bird who had flown here from the sea. None of them had ever been outside the chicken run and they were fascinated by this stranger. They nudged each other and winked and giggled. The younger ones though were shy and hid their heads beneath their wings.

They were so engrossed that they never heard Mister Farmer approaching. He had brought his shotgun with him in case Brushy Fox was about. Now he saw the commotion and ran towards the coop.

The footsteps roused Rusty and he shouted at Salty to get away. Salty didn't need to be told twice. With a last peck and a muttered thanks he flew off.

Mister Farmer saw the sudden movement. He knew Brushy Fox couldn't fly but he was convinced it was Brushy and that this was one of his tricks. In one smooth movement he raised the gun to his shoulder and fired.

Luckily for Salty he was at the end of the shotgun's range. Only a single lead pellet stung his tail. Salty wasn't badly injured, though he wouldn't be able to sit down for a week.

The fright sapped the last of his energy and he knew he would never make it to the heart of the city today. Once he reached the outskirts, he'd have to find a place to roost for the night.

Salty flew on through the afternoon and by evening he approached the lawless part of the city. Below him he saw the tumbledown houses, their gardens overgrown with weeds and littered with junk. He knew he would find no food here but what he wanted most of all was rest.

As he scanned the houses for a likely resting place, he spotted the most dilapidated house of all. And to his surprise, there on the windowsill was some food. He swooped down onto the sill and ate the crumbs. When he had eaten he peered through a chink in the plywood which blocked

up the window. It was dark in the room but as his eyes became accustomed to the gloom he saw the planks blocking the doorway.

'That's odd,' he muttered to himself. 'It's as if someone's being kept a prisoner here. But why would they leave food for the birds? These days we never come to this part of the city. Not since Timmy and Katie Goodfellow left. They were the only ones who ever fed us.'

It was a puzzle but Salty was too tired and sore to figure it out. It would be a good topic for conversation when he met his friends tomorrow though. Now he needed a night's rest and the chimney looked like a likely spot.

Salty flew up to the chimney and sure enough there was a rook's nest there. No one was home and Salty decided that Darky Rook wouldn't mind him sleeping here for the night. Salty settled himself in the nest which was soft and cosy and, mindful of his injury, composed himself for the night. Soon he was fast asleep.

As Salty settled down for the night, Timmy Goodfellow stood on the steps of the Town Hall. Just inside the doors Mister Mayor waited. Around the steps a crowd had gathered. They were awaiting the safe release of Katie Goodfellow.

As the minutes agonisingly ticked by the crowd grew

impatient. Timmy too became anxious. He scanned the street in either direction, seeking a sign of Katie. But there was none.

Mister Mayor was hopping from one leg to the other. This was a brilliant opportunity for him to make a good impression on television. All his citizens would get to see him and realise he was responsible for Katie's safe return. They would remember that at election time.

By now the crowd was becoming more impatient. They began to clap and demand that Katie be returned immediately. The police, who were keeping order, glanced at each other anxiously.

For the twentieth time Mister Mayor adjusted his robes and chain of office. He licked his lips and turned to ask one of his aides to check the street outside. Just then Mister Advisor came running towards him.

'Mister Mayor,' he gasped, 'I've just received a telephone call from Mister Kindheart. It's good news. Katie Goodfellow has been released. She's been taken to a secret address where Mister Surgeon is now examining her.'

'I've been tricked by Carbuncle,' Mister Mayor wailed. 'He's done this to humiliate me. It's intolerable. Heads will roll. Oh yes, certainly.'

'You'd best make an announcement,' Mister Advisor

suggested. 'The crowd is growing very restless. If you don't speak to them, you'll have a riot on your hands.'

'It's all so trying,' Mister Mayor cried. 'Don't they know how difficult it is to be the most important man in the city?' With that he threw back his head, thrust his chest forward and strode out onto the steps. 'Ladies and gentlemen,' he began, in his best mayoral voice, 'I have a very important announcement to make.'

'You're going to resign,' a wag called from the crowd and everyone laughed. But Timmy Goodfellow didn't join in the laughter. He was much too anxious for that. Had something gone wrong? he wondered. And where was Katie?

Timmy's anxiety was soon relieved as Mister Mayor made his announcement. The crowd cheered and Mister Mayor held up his hand.

'Naturally I'm delighted,' he said, 'that my actions have saved Katie from a terrible ordeal.'

'Saved yourself, you mean,' the wag called, and everyone laughed again. Even Timmy, who owed so much to Mister Mayor, couldn't help but smile.

Mister Mayor waved regally to the crowd and to the cameras, and went back inside the Town Hall. Timmy hesitated. He desperately wanted to see Katie but he didn't know where she was right now. He'd have to wait until she returned to Friendly Cottage. Meanwhile he decided to go along to the funfair. He could help Teddy and take his mind off things until he was reunited with Katie.

As Timmy left the steps of the Town Hall, Mister Kindheart held a meeting at his factory. It was attended by Mister Foreman and Mister Needy and some of the most trusted workers.

Mister Kindheart sat at his large oak desk. On either side of him stood Mister Savage and Mister Vicious, who had now thought better about running away. Mister Savage wore brass knuckledusters. They were stained with dried blood. Mister Vicious held a wooden club.

'These are Mister Carbuncle's thugs,' Mister Kindheart began. 'They've come here to threaten me. Normally I wouldn't allow them into my factory. But I've got no choice. I'm afraid,' he went on, his voice breaking, 'that Katie has not been released. But I've been forced to make an announcement saying she's been freed.'

At this an ugly growl went up from the gathered workers. 'Let us march on The Thieves' Den,' they shouted. One or two of them moved forward but Mister Vicious raised the club threateningly above Mister Kindheart's head.

'Please.' Mister Kindheart raised his hands. 'I'm afraid

there's nothing we can do while they've got Katie. That's why I've called this meeting. I need your help to free her.'

'We'll do anything.' Mister Needy stepped forward. He was a small man with twinkling blue eyes. But now they looked dull and pained. 'We owe so much to you,' he said. 'Our children no longer go cold and hungry. We'll do whatever you want.'

'Thank you,' Mister Kindheart said. 'I knew I could rely on you. Now let me tell you what you must do.'

Mister Kindheart outlined Mister Carbuncle's plan to destroy Toyland.

'I need you to manufacture giant aerosol cans,' he said, 'and fill them with the dangerous chemicals. Katie won't be released until we do so. Will you help me? Please. I'll pay you whatever you ask.'

Mister Foreman stepped forward, his face stern and serious.

'You are a good man,' he said. 'You are a fair employer. We know you love Katie very much. So we will help you. We will all work every hour we can so that Katie won't have to remain a prisoner for much longer. And we will not ask for a penny extra. I think I speak for all the men here.'

'Aye.' There was unanimous agreement from all present.

'Thank you,' Mister Kindheart said. 'Thank you very

much. This is something I won't forget. Now you must get to work. And do not whisper a word of this to anyone. Katie's safety depends on your co-operation and on your silence.'

With that the meeting broke up and Mister Vicious and Mister Savage returned to the Thieves' Den. Here they found Mister Carbuncle in a foul mood. Not only did he have a headache from hitting his head on the floor but he had stomach cramps from eating all the ice-cream. And he was bored.

He needed some excitement. Firstly he considered having Katie Goodfellow brought to him. He could watch while one of his henchmen removed the pins from her legs. He knew he had promised not to harm her but he had no intention of keeping that promise. Once the aerosol cans were at the North Pole he would make Katie suffer. In fact, he would demand that Timmy too be handed over to him. Then he could think of how to make them both suffer.

Of course! Mister Carbuncle had a brilliant idea and he leapt up. He'd make Timmy watch while the pins were being removed from Katie's legs. That would hurt him most of all.

Mister Carbuncle felt much better. He wanted to go out and have some fun. He remembered seeing the funfair in City Park. That was the very thing.

'Get my limousine,' he ordered. 'I'm going out to enjoy myself.'

15
A Bouncing Carbuncle

Katie Goodfellow had had a terrible day. Through every agonising minute of it she had hoped to be freed. But as the sun set she lost all hope. She had been given no more food or drink and had to sip water from the dirty cup. It was vile tasting and she had to screw up her face and hold her nose before she could swallow it. Now, as dusk fell, the water was all gone.

From time to time she had called for help. She had even tried to remove the plywood from the window. But it was tightly nailed and she couldn't budge it. The boards blocking the door were also nailed tight and the spaces between them were too narrow to crawl through.

She lay on her bed in despair. She had hoped that

Timmy would find and rescue her. But she knew no one, not even Timmy, would ever guess she was here.

She nodded off and jumped with a start when she heard a noise out on the landing. It was dark and all she could make out was a vague shadowy figure. The figure laughed and Katie recognised the malicious cackle of Mrs Haggard. Certain she was to be freed, she ran to the boarded up doorway. And it was only then she saw that Mrs Haggard had brought more food. That meant she wasn't to be freed. Katie's heart sank and a desperate sob racked her body.

'Go on, cry,' Mrs Haggard gloated. 'I just love to hear you cry.'

'You ... you have to let me go,' Katie said. 'You promised ...'

'Promises,' Mrs Haggard sneered. 'I never keep promises. Anyway, I've got my orders. Mister Carbuncle has another use for you.'

'What does he want now?' Katie asked. 'He's free, isn't he?'

'Free as a bird,' Mrs Haggard said. 'But he wants to be the richest man in the world. He's got a brilliant plan that will make us all rich. Let me tell you about it.'

Mrs Haggard recounted the plan, taking pleasure in every word. But Katie just wanted to block up her ears. It was so terribly cruel.

'He'll never get away with it,' Katie whispered. 'I don't care what he does to me. He can take the pins out of my legs if he wants. I'd prefer to be crippled rather than have him succeed.'

'It doesn't matter what you do,' Mrs Haggard taunted. 'Your foster father will comply with Mister Carbuncle's wishes. He loves you very much. That surprises me because you were always such a horrid child. If I had my way I wouldn't give you anything to eat. But I've got my orders that you're not to be harmed just now. As soon as Mister Carbuncle's plan succeeds though, I'll make you suffer.'

With that Mrs Haggard thrust the bread and water through a gap in the planks and stomped downstairs. Katie was hungry and thirsty but it was with a heavy heart that she picked up the bread and water. She ate the stale crust, keeping a little for the birds. As she pushed this through the chink, she noticed the crumbs were gone.

'A bird must have eaten them,' she thought to herself. 'If I could speak to him, he'd take a message to Timmy. I must wake early and watch for him when he comes to eat.'

Given courage by this, Katie lay down on the thin mattress and tried to sleep. But she was cold and hungry still. For hours she tossed and turned, her heart breaking at the thought of what would happen to Toyland.

At the funfair, certain that Katie was safe, Timmy was helping Teddy on the bouncing castle. Suddenly a boy ran up to Timmy and told him he'd seen Mister Carbuncle and his thugs enter the funfair. Timmy didn't believe the boy but then, as an ominous silence settled over the park, Timmy realised it was probably true. The children's whoops of joy and excitement slowly died away. Most of the rides came to a stop. The queues melted away and now there was no one to bounce on the castle. Timmy switched off the compressor and emerged from the control hut.

It was then he saw Mister Carbuncle, swaggering through the funfair. He was accompanied by Mister Vicious and two other thugs. They were laughing and pushing people out of their way.

Mister Carbuncle spotted the bouncing castle and came towards it. Timmy ducked back into the hut and watched from there.

'I think we'll try this out,' Mister Carbuncle said. 'It should be fun.'

'That'll be €2.00 for the four of you,' Teddy Needy said. 'And please take off your shoes.'

'Listen to him,' Mister Carbuncle laughed. 'He wants money from me. And asks me to take off my shoes. Even says please. Isn't he polite? Here,' he added. 'Here's my payment.' He held out his hand and when Teddy approached, Mister Carbuncle caught him by the ear. 'No one dares speak to me like that,' he growled. 'Don't you know who I am?'

'Ye ... yes, sir,' Teddy said, squirming.

'Well, don't forget it again,' Mister Carbuncle roared. He flung Teddy away and strode into the castle, followed by his thugs. 'Get this castle going,' he ordered. 'And put some bounce into it.'

Timmy switched on the compressor. Then he looked to see if Teddy was OK. Teddy was picking himself up and feeling his ear. But to Timmy's relief, he looked fine. Timmy stole a glance at the castle where Mister Carbuncle and the thugs were beginning to bounce up and down.

Timmy smiled to himself and turned back into the hut, determined to teach Mister Carbuncle a lesson. With trembling fingers he opened the valve which controlled the special bouncing gas. He watched the needle move around to the red area marked: Danger. Then he stepped outside.

It took some minutes for the gas to fill the castle. Slowly Mister Carbuncle and his thugs began to bounce higher. They squealed with pleasure and pushed and jostled each other. They never noticed they were going higher and higher.

Because Mister Carbuncle was the heaviest he bounced higher than the others. Now he reached the top of the castle.

Suddenly he realised the grave danger he was in.

'Turn off the compressor,' he cried. 'Turn it off. Turn it off.'

Timmy Goodfellow ignored his orders. Instead he watched as Mister Carbuncle went higher still, his legs and arms flailing the air. A crowd had gathered and was growing excited at the scene. Children began to applaud every bounce and when Mister Carbuncle landed on Mister Vicious and squashed him, a great cheer went up.

Mister Carbuncle went still higher. He was now soaring over the Skyrocket. Soon he was soaring above the top of the Big Wheel. He could be seen all about the fair.

'It's a killer whale,' some people said. 'It's leaping for fish.'

'First killer whale with arms and legs that I've seen,' someone else joked.

'Look,' another said. 'Whatever it is, it's going higher.'

This was so. Mister Carbuncle was now shooting 100 feet into the air. The other thugs had seen the danger and as they weren't bouncing so high, climbed down off the castle. Now they stood laughing with the crowd while Mister Carbuncle bounced all alone.

No one can ever say what might have happened if it hadn't been for a gust of wind. Perhaps Mister Carbuncle would have gone into space and would be orbiting the earth right now. But a gust of wind came at just the right moment.

Mister Carbuncle, high in the air above the castle, was caught by the wind. It hurled him through the air and he landed in a tangle of arms and legs in the candyfloss machine.

Immediately he stopped bouncing and began to whirl around. Round and round he whirled until he was wrapped from head to foot in candyfloss. The crowd roared with laughter and Timmy and Teddy couldn't help but laugh too.

Just then Mister Vicious arrived at a run. He grabbed the hammer from The Test Your Strength Meter and smashed the motor on the candyfloss machine. It stopped turning and Mister Vicious helped Mister Carbuncle get off.

The Boss of The Underworld was staggering and feeling queasy. Everything was spinning around.

'Take me home,' he mumbled. 'I must lie down.'

Mister Vicious led him and the other thugs towards the gate. Timmy, Teddy and the laughing, jeering crowd followed them. As the thugs walked through the park they passed beneath an oak tree. In the fork of a branch, a colony of wasps had built a nest.

The wasps smelled the candyfloss and became excited. They swarmed out of the nest and attacked Mister Carbuncle. The last Timmy Goodfellow saw of the crooks was the four of them, running for their lives, pursued by the wasps. It was, he decided, the funniest thing he'd seen in a very long time.

16
Timmy Learns the Truth

Timmy was in good spirits as he hurried home from the funfair. What a story he had for Katie! But as he entered the kitchen at home he knew something was wrong. His foster parents were sitting alone at the table. There was no sign of Katie.

His foster mother turned towards him. She smiled, but the emotion never touched her eyes.

'Hello, Timmy,' she said, and burst into tears.

'What's wrong?' he asked. 'Is ... is it Katie?'

'Sit down, Timmy,' Mister Kindheart said. 'We've something to tell you.' He looked tired and there were bags beneath his eyes. With a heavy heart Timmy sat and for some moments there was an ominous silence in the room.

Then Mister Kindheart told Timmy the awful truth. Timmy sat stunned. He couldn't believe what he'd heard. It couldn't be so. Mister Carbuncle had promised. But then he realised that the crook's word couldn't be trusted.

'I must see Mister Mayor right away,' he said, getting to his feet. 'He'll get Mister Inspector to re-double his efforts to find Katie.'

'No,' Mister Kindheart warned. 'We mustn't tell anyone. The only way we can save Katie is to do as Mister Carbuncle asks. Once the aerosol cans are at the North Pole, he'll free Katie.'

'But what about Toyland?' Timmy said. 'And my friend Santa? If anything happens to Toyland it'll break his heart. He's an old man you know. Toyland is his whole life.'

'We know that, Timmy,' Mrs Kindheart said, wiping her eyes. 'But we must think of Katie first. She is your sister.'

'I know,' Timmy said. 'I'm sorry. But I care about Santa too. If only we could help both of them.'

'Well, we can't,' Mister Kindheart said. 'We must do as Mister Carbuncle asks. Once Katie's free, we'll inform the police and they can deal with the thugs. You understand, don't you, Timmy?'

Through his misery, Timmy could only nod. In his heart he knew that Mister Carbuncle might not keep his word.

He was a cruel man who loved to see people suffer. When the cans were safely at the North Pole, he might still remove the pins from Katie's legs. Timmy realised that Katie's safety might depend entirely on him. Somehow he had to find her before it was too late. But he must do so secretly.

'I must be off to the factory,' Mister Kindheart said, trying to sound cheerful. 'I have to ensure the late shift is operating satisfactorily.'

'How long will it take to make the cans?' Timmy asked.

'About two days,' Mister Kindheart said. 'Everyone at the factory is helping me. They're working sixteen hours a day.'

Timmy nodded and asked to be excused. He went upstairs to his room and lay on his bed. Somehow he had to find Katie in the next 48 hours. But how could he find her? Mousey and Ratty had drawn a complete blank. She wasn't hidden anywhere in the city. Every nook and cranny had been checked.

For ages Timmy lay awake before coming to a decision. In the morning he'd go to The Thieves' Den and spy on the thugs. Perhaps that way he'd learn where Katie was hidden.

Timmy slept badly that night and was awake at dawn. He leapt from his bed and hurriedly washed and dressed. He was about to go downstairs when he heard a tap on the window.

He looked out to see a worried looking Chalky Crow

sitting on the sill. Timmy opened the window to say hello to his friend.

'I just heard the news, Timmy,' Chalky said. 'It's terrible. Terrible.' He blinked and sniffed. 'I came to offer help,' he added. 'If there's anything I or my friends can do for you, please say.'

'Thanks,' Timmy replied. 'But Mousey and Ratty have had the city searched. They found no trace of Katie.'

Chalky nodded. 'She must be hidden in the country-side,' he said. 'That's our territory. I'll have every bird scouring the countryside for her within the hour. Mind you, Beaky Blackbird is away on his travels at the moment. He may have some news when he returns. If Katie's out there, Timmy, we'll find her. Now keep your spirits up.'

It was Timmy's turn to nod. He was overwhelmed by the kindness of all his friends.

'I'll be off,' Chalky said. 'There's no time to lose.'

Chalky flew off and Timmy rushed downstairs. He hurriedly ate his breakfast and set off for The Thieves' Den to spy on the crooks as he'd planned.

Salty Seagull was also awake at dawn. He was sore and stiff, and gingerly stood up. When he'd eased his muscles, he set about preening his feathers. Once this was done, his thoughts turned to breakfast. He wondered if there might be more bread on the windowsill and he flew down to investigate. A tiny piece had been left there and Salty ate it gratefully.

He was curious about his benefactor and peeped into the room through the chink. But he could only see a part of the room. It seemed to be unoccupied. But why then were those planks nailed across the doorway? Surely they were intended to keep someone a prisoner, someone who was thoughtful enough to give some of their meagre rations to him.

Salty was about to peck the plywood when he heard someone on the stairs. He saw Mrs Haggard appear at the door. She had a piece of bread in one hand and a cup of water in the other. So there was a prisoner here ...

Mrs Haggard placed the bread and water on the floor.

'Breakfast time,' she laughed. 'Lovely stale bread and stagnant water. I got it specially from a puddle in the yard.'

Salty was angered by this. How dare anyone do such a thing! Well, he'd see to it that something was done. When this horrid woman went away he'd ensure that he spoke with the prisoner.

But just then something struck the plywood beside Salty's head. He swung round and spotted a boy with a catapult in the next yard. Salty didn't hesitate. He literally threw himself off the windowsill and dived downwards. But even so he was a split second too late. The boy's second stone struck him on the breast, momentarily winding him.

Gasping for air he found himself dropping like a stone towards the ground. Death or serious injury faced him and he knew that only his experience could save him now. He spread his wings, angling them to give maximum lift and breaking power. He was but inches from the ground and could see the scum on the puddles, when he pulled out of the dive. He skimmed across the yard and over the broken fence into the waste ground beyond. There were some bushes in the distance and, with a desperate struggle, Salty made it there.

He knew he was lucky to be alive, though he wouldn't be able to fly very far today. He would have to complete his journey in stages. Slowly he recovered and when he did so, his thoughts strayed to the prisoner. He dare not return now to speak to whoever was in that room. The boy with the catapult was much too accurate for comfort. He would speak with his friends though about the prisoner. Perhaps they might know who it was.

If only Salty knew that at that very moment the prisoner was staring from the chink in the window. Katie thought at first that it was a bird who'd made the noise. She didn't stop to think that a bird could not have made such a loud noise. As she looked out she saw Salty skim the top of the fence and also spotted the boy with the catapult. She rapped on the plywood to alert the boy's attention. But he thought it was Mrs Haggard who was at the window, and he took to his heels and ran away.

Katie was in despair. The bird who might have helped her had flown away and would not return. It would be too frightened of the boy with the catapult. Her only chance of alerting Timmy had gone.

Katie returned to the bed, threw herself down on it and wept. By the door Mrs Haggard laughed. Her manic cackle followed her as she went downstairs. And for ages afterwards it echoed in Katie's ears.

17
Many Developments

Through the morning Salty Seagull huddled in the bush. He was bruised but there was no permanent damage. At noon he felt he'd recovered sufficiently to continue his journey. But he could only remain on the wing for short periods.

Late in the afternoon he left the lawless area of the city and landed in a garden which had a bird table. Here he took much needed refreshments before perching in a tree to rest.

It was here Beaky Blackbird, returning from his travels, found him. Salty recounted his adventures for his friend who listened with open beak.

'That boy could have killed you,' Beaky said angrily. 'You were lucky to escape.'

'I know,' Salty said. 'Unlike that unfortunate prisoner. I

wonder who it could be.'

'I don't know,' Beaky said. 'And I don't want to go there to find out. That boy won't give up easily.'

Salty nodded and shivered, and Beaky felt great sympathy for his him.

'Come on,' he said now, wanting to take the seagull's mind off what had happened. 'Let's go on. I'll fly with you to ensure you're OK.'

'Thanks,' Salty said. 'You're a true friend.'

With that the two birds took to the wing and headed east across the city, stopping to rest whenever Salty felt tired. By Beaky's reckoning, they'd reach home before dark.

That same day, while Timmy spied on The Thieves' Den from a derelict house across the street, a meeting was held in the operations' room. Mister Carbuncle presided and the meeting was attended by Mister Brains, an expert on everything. He wanted to be rich and so he sold his services to crooks for large sums of money.

'Well Brains?' Mister Carbuncle said. 'How do you suggest we get the cans to the North Pole?'

'We transport them by lorry to the airport,' Mister Brains suggested. 'From there we fly them to the North Pole and drop them by parachute.'

'I want to be there,' Mister Carbuncle pleaded. 'I want to see Toyland destroyed and Santa Claus and his elves floating in the icy sea.'

'Me too. Me too,' the other thugs echoed.

'But do you want to jump from a plane?' Mister Carbuncle asked. 'What if something happened to your parachute?'

At this the thugs grew silent. They were cruel men but they were cowards at heart. They were frightened of any danger befalling themselves. Mister Carbuncle laughed at their discomfiture.

'You don't like that,' he scoffed, forgetting of course that he himself was more of a coward than anyone.

'You could fly to the arctic,' Mister Brains suggested now. 'From there you could travel to the North Pole on a sleigh.'

'Yes,' the other thugs chortled. 'Let's do that.'

'OK,' Mister Carbuncle sneered. 'You can travel the cowards way.' But he was secretly relieved. He didn't fancy jumping from a plane either.

'We'll need someone at the North Pole,' Mister Brains said, 'to mark the spot where the pilot has to drop the cans. Someone will also have to provide the sleigh and drive it. After all, you won't know your way to the pole. Nor can you handle a team of huskies.'

'Now I suggest we ask Icy, the Wicked Witch of the

North, for assistance,' Mister Brains continued. 'She hates Santa Claus. She'll help us and we won't have to pay her.'

'Goody,' Mister Carbuncle chortled. He hated having to pay for anything and even now was trying to figure out a way of not paying Mister Brains. After all, he could have thought of all this himself.

'I'll summon her then,' Mister Brains said. 'She can be here this evening. She no longer travels by broomstick. She's now got a jet engined vacuum cleaner which can fly at 1,000 miles an hour. You could fly to the North Pole with her if you liked,' he suggested to Mister Carbuncle.

'Who'd watch them?' Mister Carbuncle waved at his thugs and hoped none of them suspected the truth. He was too scared to fly on a vacuum cleaner with a witch. And probably her black cat as well. Witches always had black cats with green staring eyes and horrible personalities. How could he fly through the air at 1,000 miles an hour with them? Mister Carbuncle shivered at the thought.

But Mr Carbuncle quickly recovered and glared about him. He glared particularly hard at Mister Brains. He suspected that the expert was trying to make a fool of him. When this was over he would make Mister Brains pay. He would ask Icy Witch to take him for a ride on her vacuum cleaner – without a safety belt, of course. That would teach him.

The whole episode put Mister Carbuncle in a foul mood.

'I must lie down,' he wailed. 'My poor head hurts from all this thinking.'

With that he stumbled off to his dark bedroom and lay down on his giant bed. Soon he was asleep and dreaming once more of untold riches.

Salty and Beaky reached home as darkness fell. Their friends were settling down for the night, tired after their fruitless search for Katie Goodfellow. But rumours about Salty's adventures were soon buzzing about. The birds couldn't sleep and so they gathered around Salty to hear his story. When he spoke of the prisoner, Chalky Crow interrupted.

'It must be Katie Goodfellow who's the prisoner,' he cawed, hopping about on the branch of the tree. 'And that woman is Mrs Haggard. That's why the rats and mice never found Katie. No mouse or rat ever goes in there anymore.'

'What do we do now?' Chirpy Sparrow asked.

'We must inform Timmy,' Chalky said. 'There's no time to lose.'

'I'll go,' Hooty Owl said. 'After all, I'm well used to flying in the dark.'

'Timmy's spying on The Thieves' Den,' Chalky said.

'You'll find him there. Now hurry back. We'll all be anxious for news.'

'Good speed,' the others echoed and they listened intently until the beat of Hooty's wings faded. Then they perched in silence waiting for his return.

18
Mousey in Peril

All day Timmy had spied on The Thieves' Den but had learned nothing new. At sunset he went home, hungry and disillusioned. After supper he went to his room and lay on his bed. He was trying to figure out where Katie might be when he heard Hooty Owl calling him. Timmy ran to the window and opened it.

'Thank goodness you're here,' Hooty said, breathlessly. 'I've been searching for you at The Thieves' Den. Now have I got news for you!' Hooty hopped with excitement. 'We've found Katie. She's being held prisoner by Mrs Haggard.'

'No!' Timmy wailed. 'Not Mrs Haggard. Oh, poor Katie.'

'Let me tell you what's happened,' Hooty said, and he

told Timmy the story.

'I must go to her at once,' Timmy said.

'Hold on,' Hooty warned. 'You can't go blundering in there. Mrs Haggard will be vigilant. First of all, we need someone to slip in quietly and reconnoitre the situation.'

'Mousey,' Timmy said quietly. 'Mousey knows that house inside out.'

'The very man,' Hooty said. 'I'll go and get him. I know where he'll be just now. Him and Ratty meet each evening to play poker and have a pint or two. I'll be as quick as I can.'

Timmy nodded and watched as Hooty flashed off into the darkness. He stood by the window waiting, his anxiety building up with every passing minute.

Mister Carbuncle woke with a headache. He was still angry with Mister Brains and wanted someone to suffer. Well, the ideal victim was Katie Goodfellow. He'd remove the pins from her legs and send them to her brother. Impatient to put his idea into practise, he summoned Mister Vicious.

'Bring Katie Goodfellow here immediately,' Mister Carbuncle ordered. 'I need some fun so I've decided to remove the pins right away. So find me a pincers and light a coal fire. I want to redden the pincers before I use them.'

'I'll have her brought right away,' Mister Vicious said. 'Can I help?' he added. 'Maybe I could pull out one of the pins.'

'Oh, no,' Mister Carbuncle said. 'This is my fun. Now go and get her. And make sure the pincers have sharp jaws. I want a good hot fire too. Use only the best coal.'

'Yes, sir,' Mister Vicious said, and he backed out of the room.

By now Mousey had been briefed by Timmy and was on his way to Mrs Haggard's. Ratty had insisted on going along too because he felt responsible for not having located Katie. After all, he was the one who had forgotten that he had once warned the rats not to go into Mrs Haggard's house.

'Old age,' he'd muttered shamefaced. 'My brain isn't what it used to be.'

It was a tiring journey for old timers and they stopped a few times to rest. But anxiety pushed them on and eventually they reached their destination.

'I'll keep guard,' Ratty whispered, 'while you go in. If you're not out in ten minutes I'm coming in. Now take care.'

Mousey nodded and, clapping Ratty on the shoulder, slipped away. Mousey had lived here in Timmy's and Katie's time and he knew the house like the back of his paw.

Making his way to the rear of the house, he entered through a hole in the rotting kitchen door.

He crept across the kitchen, avoiding a trap, the teeth of which gleamed in the dim light, and entered the hall. From the living room he heard the sound of the television and Mrs Haggard's cackle as she laughed. Mousey hesitated before slipping upstairs to the attic.

There were three traps here, one of which was large enough to catch a child. It was chained to the wall and its teeth had been newly filed. Anyone caught in those gaping jaws would never escape.

Mousey's whiskers quivered but he fought his fear. Gathering his courage, he slipped into Katie's room. His eyes were now accustomed to the gloom and he saw Katie curled up in a ball on the bed.

Mousey tiptoed across the room and gently touched Katie's cheek with his paw. Her skin was wet and Mousey realised she had been crying. For a moment he was over-whelmed with both sadness and anger. How could anyone do such a terrible thing to a little girl? He knew that mice would never do such a thing to one of their own.

Again Mousey touched Katie's cheek and she opened her eyes.

'Sshhh,' Mousey warned. 'Don't make a sound.'

'Mousey!' Katie whispered. 'Is it you?'

'Yes,' Mousey replied. 'It's me.'

'What are you doing here?' Katie asked. 'How did you find me?'

'I'll tell you everything later,' Mousey said. 'Now we must get out of here.'

'Oh, I'm so glad to see you,' Katie whispered. 'I've been so frightened.'

She reached out and stroked Mousey's grey head. Her touch was soft and gentle and Mousey could have stayed there all night. But there were urgent matters to attend to. He shook himself and stood back.

'I have to get you out of here,' he said. 'And as quickly as possible. Now let me see.' Mousey scratched his head and his whiskers quivered as he concentrated. He nodded and looked up at Katie. 'I think ...' he began but got no further.

Just then a vehicle screeched to a stop outside. A moment later there was a loud rapping on the front door. Voices could be heard and the clump of heavy boots on the stairs. A bulb on the landing was switched on and Mousey and Katie saw the newcomers. They were Mister Carbuncle's thugs, led by Mister Vicious and Mister Savage. A tremor ran through Mousey's body. He'd come too late.

The thugs tore down the planks with jemmies.

'Get the girl,' Mister Vicious ordered. 'The Boss is anxious to meet her. He has a pincers reddening in a fire right now. We don't want them going cold.'

'Eeekk!' Mousey couldn't help giving a squeak of alarm.

'What's that?' Mister Vicious entered the room, his jemmy held threateningly aloft.

'It sounded like a mouse to me.' Mrs Haggard had come upstairs. 'But they don't normally come in here because of the traps. She and her horrid brother were friendly with the rats and mice though.'

'Guard the door,' Mister Vicious ordered. 'If there's a mouse here we'll kill it. We mustn't let it escape to raise the alarm.'

Mister Savage, Mrs Haggard and the other thugs stood guard by the door. Mister Vicious advanced with caution, his eyes darting here and there. By now Mousey had slipped down by the side of the mattress. His heart pounded in terror. He'd lived a long, fruitful life but this looked like the end. He'd die here, failing the friends who had been so good to him over the years.

Katie too was paralysed with fear. She knew Mousey would be unlikely to escape with his life. Even the threat of the red-hot pincers didn't bother her as much as the threat of Mousey's likely death.

Mister Vicious' shadow now loomed menacingly on the

wall, the jemmy raised above his head. His breathing was slow and measured. Mousey tried to burrow under the mattress. But Mister Vicious detected the rustling noise. With a whoop that made Mousey's fur stand on end, the thug leapt forward to deal the blow which would crush Mousey's brains.

But before Mister Vicious could deliver the fatal blow Mrs Haggard screamed. It was a high-pitched scream of terror and it paralysed the thugs with fear. Mrs Haggard screamed again and began to hop about, her heavy boots beating out a rhythm that defied counting.

Pandemonium broke out. The thugs began to jump about too. They thought Mrs Haggard had seen a ghost. Only Mister Vicious kept his head. He swung about, and it was he who spotted Ratty clinging to Mrs Haggard's stocking, nibbling her leg. Ratty had followed the thugs into the house and, thinking that Mister Vicious was about to hit Katie with the jemmy, in anger and distraction attacked the nearest person to him. This was Mrs Haggard.

Mister Vicious ran forward and swung the jemmy at Ratty. But Ratty was too quick for him and leapt away. The jemmy struck Mrs Haggard on the knee and she jumped three feet in the air.

Ratty leapt onto Mister Savage's shoulder. Mister Vicious swung the jemmy again but once more Ratty was too quick for him. The blow missed him and struck Mister Savage's ear. He screamed with rage and pain, and attacked Mister Vicious. The two thugs fell wrestling on the floor. The other thugs took to their heels and ran away. Meanwhile, Mrs Haggard still hopped around on one leg.

Mousey had crept out of his hiding place. Now he saw his chance. He scrabbled onto Katie's shoulder.

'Come on,' he urged in her ear. 'This is your chance to getaway.'

Katie didn't need urging. She leapt to her feet and rushed to the door. Ratty was on the landing, beckoning her with his paw while Mousey was hot on her heels. The two struggling thugs were unaware of what was happening.

But Mrs Haggard was more alert. As Katie dashed through the doorway Mrs Haggard grabbed her by the hair and pulled her back. Katie struggled to escape but Mrs Haggard's grip was firm.

'Get away!' Katie screamed at Mousey and Ratty. 'Go and warn Timmy. He'll know what to do.'

Mousey and Ratty hesitated. They didn't want to leave Katie. But they knew they could do nothing now. As Mrs Haggard kicked the two wrestling thugs with her heavy boots and ordered them to get up, Mousey and Ratty slipped down-stairs and hid in a corner to see what would happen now.

'We have to get out of here,' they heard Mrs Haggard cry. 'The mouse and rat will raise the alarm. Then this place will be crawling with police.'

'We'll go back to The Thieves' Den,' Mister Vicious said. 'We'll take you and the girl with us. Mister Carbuncle will find her a new hiding place.'

The thugs bundled Katie down the stairs. Mrs Haggard followed them.

'We must warn Timmy immediately,' Mousey said as he and Ratty slipped out of the house. 'I only hope we're not too late. There's no knowing what Mister Carbuncle will do now.'

'I know,' Ratty said, and with a final glance about, they set off for the long journey back to Friendly Cottage.

19
The Wicked Witch

That same evening The Wicked Witch of the North arrived in the city. She came on her jet-engined vacuum cleaner, trailing vapour and flame behind her. At the airport an air traffic controller watched her arrive on his radar screen. He knew of her reputation and allowed her to proceed.

She circled the city while the residents watched with trepidation. She was the personification of evil, and ill-luck followed her wherever she went.

'She's heading for the lawless parts,' people whispered in fear. 'Maybe she intends to team up with Mister Carbuncle. If she does, we're doomed.'

Icy heard them and cackled with pleasure. Her travelling machine was fitted with loudspeakers and her laughter echoed through the city. At the Town Hall Mister Mayor convened an emergency meeting of the City Council. The police were placed on alert.

Still cackling, Icy swooped down into the courtyard of The Thieves' Den and was taken immediately to meet Mister Carbuncle. She was the only person on earth Mister Carbuncle feared and he was on his best behaviour. He called her Madam Icy and thanked her for coming. He outlined his plan to destroy Toyland and asked for her help.

'It will be the end of Santa Claus,' Mister Carbuncle added, playing his trump card.

'If that's so,' Icy said gloatingly, 'I'm willing to help. But I want Santa Claus and his elves handed over to me. I'll make them work night and day to make toys that are faulty. Then next Christmas I'll make Santa deliver them to every child in the world. On Christmas morning he'll be the most hated person on earth. Even I'll have to take second place. That naturally upsets me but it will compensate me to know that Santa will never be loved again.'

'I like it,' Mister Carbuncle chortled. 'I want revenge on Santa Claus too. And on a boy and girl who live here in the city. In fact the girl is on her way here now. I have a pincers reddening in a fire in my torture chamber beneath the building. You can watch me punish this girl if you like.'

'I'd love to,' the witch said. 'I'll help if you want.'

'Oh no,' Mister Carbuncle said. 'This is my fun. Listen,' he added, 'I hear them arriving. Come along. You'll see how we punish people here.'

Mister Carbuncle rubbed his hands together and rushed out of the operations' room. Icy followed him down the wet stone steps to an underground cavern beneath The Thieves' Den. It was cut out of rock and the walls dripped with moisture.

Here were the tickling machines, Mister Carbuncle's terrible instruments of torture. One machine was fitted with feathers which tickled the soles of the feet. Another ticked under the armpits. But the most terrible one of all tickled all over. Here men were known to scream for mercy. Anyone who'd been tortured had never laughed again.

In the centre of the cavern floor a huge coal fire burned. In the depths of the fire a pincers was reddening. It glowed in the gloom and sparks flew from it.

While Mister Carbuncle stared lovingly at the pincers, Katie was thrust into the room by Mister Vicious. Mister Carbuncle laughed when he saw her fear. He caught her by the hair and dragged her to the fire, showing her the pincers.

'Hold her,' he ordered his henchman. 'I can hardly wait.'

'Bo ... Boss,' Mister Vicious stuttered. 'We're in trouble.'

'What?' Mister Carbuncle released Katie and swung around. 'What do you mean by trouble?'

Stuttering and mumbling, Mister Vicious explained what had happened.

'Timmy Goodfellow is probably on his way here already,' he finished. 'He'll bring the police down on us. We've got to get away.'

'Get away!' Mister Carbuncle screamed. 'And let my brilliant plan fail? I'll have you tortured for suggesting such a thing.'

'Please,' Mister Vicious begged. 'Not the tickling machine.'

'There's no time for this,' Icy witch said. 'And I don't want my chance for revenge against Santa Claus ruined. Let me see. Yes. I think it's the only solution. But I'll have to have someone to look after her. I couldn't bear to do it myself.'

'What are you suggesting, Madam Icy?' Mister Carbuncle asked.

'I'll take that ... that girl back with me to the North Pole,' Icy Witch said. 'No one will ever find her there.'

'Splendid,' Mister Carbuncle clapped. 'It's perfect. I was about to suggest it myself.'

'Stuff and nonsense,' the witch exclaimed. 'You don't have a single idea in that lump of soggy porridge you call your brain. I've got to do all the thinking. Now, I'll need someone to look after her.'

'Mrs Haggard could do it,' Mister Vicious suggested, trying to get back into his Boss' good books.

'Fine,' Icy said. 'Now, take this girl upstairs. There's no time to lose. I must leave immediately for the North Pole. I'll use my after burner for maximum speed. I can only carry one passenger. So I'll have to return for this Haggard woman.'

Icy Witch whirled about and strode out of the dungeon. Mister Vicious caught Katie, dragging her upstairs and out to the flying machine where she was strapped on behind Icy Witch. Then with a roar and a spurt of flame the machine roared into the sky. Banking sharply, it headed north towards the cold bleak wastes of the arctic.

*A*t that moment Timmy Goodfellow was hurrying through the city towards The Thieves' Den. Mousey and Ratty had told him what had happened and he had decided to try and rescue Katie before Mister Carbuncle could hurt her.

As he hurried on alone he heard a whooshing noise above his head. Looking up he saw Icy Witch whiz across the sky, flames trailing from her machine. She was travelling at great speed and soon crossed the face of the moon. As she did so, Timmy clearly saw that there were two people on the machine. The person sitting behind the witch was much smaller. He knew it had to be his sister.

'Katie!' Timmy called her name aloud. 'Katie! Katie!' he called again and again until the flying machine vanished from sight.

For a long time he stood staring up at the sky seeking another glimpse of his sister. But the sky remained empty. He stayed until the cold seeped into his bones.

In fact he might stayed there all night if Hooty Owl hadn't seen him. Hooty had seen the witch arrive in the city and had followed her. He had witnessed the happenings at The Thieves' Den and was again following the witch when he spotted Timmy.

Hooty swooped down and perched on Timmy's shoulder telling him what had happened. 'What are you going to do now?' he asked.'

'There's nothing I can do,' Timmy said sadly. 'It's too late. How can I ever rescue Katie from the wastes of the arctic? I don't suppose I'll ever see her again.'

'There's still a chance,' Hooty said. 'Icy Witch is going to return for Mrs Haggard. If you could force her to take you with her, you might be able to rescue Katie.'

'I can try,' Timmy said.

'It'll be dangerous,' Hooty warned. 'Icy Witch has great powers.'

'I know,' Timmy said. 'But I must try. I can't leave Katie to her fate. Now I'd best hurry to The Thieves' Den. I have to be ready when the witch comes for Mrs Haggard. As you say, it's my only hope.'

Timmy set off again for The Thieves' Den. He knew he was facing more danger than he had ever faced before. But he summoned up his courage and hurried on.

20
A Prickly Situation

In different circumstances Katie might have enjoyed her flight. But the knowledge that she was heading for the arctic and might never return spoiled any pleasure there might have been. She whizzed through the air at enormous speed, the stars no more than a blur. The wind whistled past her ears with an unending shriek that set her teeth on edge.

It grew colder and Katie's teeth chattered. Her hands and feet became numbed and if she hadn't been strapped on she would have fallen off. Her cheeks and fingers turned blue and tears sprang up in her eyes. The tears welled up on her eyelids but before they could tumble off, they froze.

From time to time she glanced down. Far below she could see the ice gleaming in the moonlight, stretching as far as the eye could see. In some places it was flat and featureless. In others it was sculpted into fantastic shapes, as if by giants.

Icy Witch banked her flying machine and Katie saw the glow of the Milky Way. It consisted of billions of stars. They were of every colour known on earth and some that were as yet unknown. As they drew near, Katie realised they spelled a word: Toyland.

Her heart lurched in her chest as if it had torn itself free. Out there were Santa Claus and the elves. Katie couldn't take her eyes from the sign which now seemed to fill the night sky. She felt a warm thrill flow through her at the thought that Santa was so close.

Katie was so engrossed that she didn't notice that they were dropping out of the sky until she felt dampness on her cheek. Her frozen tears were melting. Now, below, she saw the witch's palace. It was black and stood out in the vast whiteness. It was monstrous and ugly and Katie turned her head to look back. But she could no longer see the magical glow of Toyland.

They landed within the palace walls and immediately four goblins skated out to meet them. They bowed to the witch who ordered them to lock Katie in the tower.

'Ensure she doesn't escape,' Icy said. 'Otherwise you'll end up in my cauldron.' She gave her manic cackle and with a whoosh of flame, flew off into the night.

The goblins, who were dressed in suits of fur stolen from polar bears, now dragged Katie to the tower. It was 300 feet high and contained countless tiny windows. Once inside she was handed over to Goblin Jailer who took her to a cell and locked her in. The cell was small with one of those tiny windows high up in the wall. The door was made of steel bars. Beneath the window was a narrow ledge.

As the steel door clanged shut behind her Katie felt a surge of despair. She crossed to the ledge and threw herself down on it. It was cold and slippery, and only then did she realise it was made of ice. She got up and felt the walls of her cell. They were built of blocks of ice too, which had been dyed black. They had magical properties and so did not melt easily.

After examining her cell, Katie stared up at the window. She could see a single star in the sky. It glowed brightly and she realised it was the North Star. Watching it, she thought of her snug bed in Friendly Cottage. Would she ever sleep in it again? Would she ever see Timmy or her foster parents again? Would this cell be her prison forever and ever?

She knew that those who were imprisoned by the Wicked Witch never escaped. Here in this tower, behind each of those tiny windows, there was a prisoner like herself. Here they probably stood as she did, watching the North

Star and thinking of their homes and their families and wondering, as she did, if they would ever see them again.

Once Katie left for the North Pole, the thugs at The Thieves' Den relaxed. Most of them stood about in the courtyard awaiting the return of the witch. The main gate had not been repaired since the police broke it down and so Timmy Goodfellow was able to slip unnoticed into the courtyard.

Timmy hid behind a rusting security van Mister Carbuncle had once robbed, and waited. From here he could see Mrs Haggard. She was wearing three coats and two hats and had three scarves wrapped about her neck. She'd torn a blanket into strips and these were wrapped about her legs. On her hands she wore thick woollen gloves.

Seeing her, Timmy realised he was poorly equipped for the journey. But there was little he could do about it now. He would have to brave the cold as Katie did. Thinking of Katie made Timmy angry and, as the warm blood rushed through his veins, he forgot about the ordeal he would soon face.

Just then Timmy heard the whoosh of the jet engine and looked up to see the witch coming in to land again. Timmy was poised to attack and never took his eyes from the machine as it landed in the centre of the courtyard.

As Mrs Haggard waddled forward Timmy took a deep breath. All his anger and frustration materialised in a scream as he charged across the cobbles. His sudden appearance froze the thugs on the spot. They were unable to move. Mrs Haggard too hesitated. She was convinced Timmy was a demon who had come for her. Even the witch was temporarily paralysed by it all.

Timmy's plan might have succeeded but for oil spilled on the cobbles. As he raced across the yard he slipped and momentarily lost his footing. As he struggled to regain his balance Mrs Haggard realised who it was. Relieved it wasn't a demon, she waddled to the flying machine and climbed on board. Her bulky clothing made this difficult and the delay gave Timmy some valuable seconds.

As Mrs Haggard seated herself, Timmy reached the machine. The witch opened the throttle and flame spurted from the rear nozzle. As the machine lifted off, Timmy grabbed the tail of one of Mrs Haggard's coats. This unbalanced Mrs Haggard, who grabbed the witch to prevent herself falling off. This in turn unbalanced both the witch and the flying machine. It banked sharply and Mrs Haggard slipped further. But then the power of the machine wrenched the coat tail from Timmy's grip. The machine shot into the sky, with Mrs Haggard hanging on for dear life, screeching for help.

The witch wrestled with the controls. The machine banked one way and then the other. Mrs Haggard was flung about, her coat tails flailing behind her. One of her hats flew off and she made a grab for it.

It was a foolish thing to do. The machine banked again at that moment and Mrs Haggard fell off. She fell in a whirl of arms and legs and landed in a thorn bush at the end of the street. Despite her bulky clothing, the thorns prodded her everywhere. As she threshed about, the thorns went deeper and deeper until she resembled a pin cushion.

While she howled in pain the thugs laughed and clapped each other on the back. Timmy Goodfellow took the opportunity to escape and dashed from the courtyard. From the street he watched the witch regain control of her flying machine. Now she swooped down and hovered above the thorn bush. Mrs Haggard reached up and grabbed the safely belt, pulling herself on board. With a whoosh of flame the machine shot into the sky.

Timmy could only stand and watch until it disappeared in the distance. With a heavy heart he set off for home, his footsteps echoing in the quiet city. On and on he plodded, his only thought being that he might never see Katie again.

21
Timmy's Brilliant Idea

When Timmy arrived home his foster parents were waiting for him. He informed them of what had happened but they did not admonish him. They knew he loved Katie and had acted with the best intentions.

'We must carry out Mister Carbuncle's wishes,' Mister Kindheart said. 'I'm afraid we've got no choice now. Katie is now out of reach of the police. There's no way to rescue her.

'The aerosol cans will be ready tomorrow,' he continued. 'They'll be taken to the airport and flown from there to the North Pole, where they'll be dropped by parachute.'

'Is Mister Carbuncle travelling with the cans?' Timmy asked.

'No,' Mister Kindheart said. 'He's frightened of parachute

jumping. He and his thugs are flying there in a special plane fitted with skis instead of wheels. It can land and take off from the ice. They're going to land near the witch's palace and travel onto the North Pole by sleigh. I overheard Mister Vicious discussing it all.'

'Now don't worry, Timmy,' Mister Kindheart added. 'We've ceased production on everything else. No shaving foam or furniture polish or deodorant has been filled into a single can since Mister Carbuncle's demands were made. Even Teddy Needy has come to help us. He wanted to help when his father told him what had happened.'

Timmy was moved by this. But it got him no closer to rescuing Katie or thwarting Mister Carbuncle's plan to destroy Toyland. Through the night no solution came to him. In the morning, after breakfast, he announced that he was going to meet Teddy Needy. He needed someone to talk to.

Timmy found Teddy at home. He was preparing to go to the factory to help in the manufacture of the cans.

'Come with me, Timmy,' he said. 'You can help too, you know. And try not to worry,' he added. 'Everyone's doing their best to help. The workmen are working round the clock. I've been helping myself. I'm small enough to climb inside the cans and polish them. You could do that job too. Come on, Timmy. Come and help me.'

'OK,' Timmy agreed. 'I'll come and help.'

'Let's go, then,' Teddy said, and they raced to the factory.

Inside the factory there was a tremendous din. Giant guillotines cut sheets of steel which were shaped into cylinders by other machines. These were then welded to form giant cans. Welding torches arced and gave off a brilliant blue flame. In their welding masks the workmen looked like robots from an alien planet.

In another part of the factory other workers were making giant nozzles for the cans. Others were bringing welding rods to the welders and ensuring that the whole operation ran smoothly.

'This way, Timmy,' Teddy called above the din. 'These cans here are ready for polishing.' Teddy led Timmy to the end of the factory where a number of shiny cylinders lay on trestles. Teddy handed his friend polishing cloths and polish.

'Climb into the can,' he explained. 'Polish as you go. When the polishing is complete, workmen will weld on the bottom of the can.'

Timmy took the cloths and polish and climbed into a can. It was just large enough to accommodate him and he polished every inch of it as he crawled along its length. It was hot and stuffy in the confined space but Timmy put up with the discomfort.

As he moved to the next can Timmy had a brilliant idea. It seemed crazy and dangerous at first. But the more he thought about it, the more excited he became. If he could persuade some of the workmen to help him, then he could put his idea into action.

Trembling with excitement and anticipation, Timmy went in search of Mister Needy. He found him busily directing the welders. Timmy beckoned him and Mister Needy came to join him. In a quiet corner, Timmy outlined his plan.

Mister Needy was dumbfounded by it. He was fearful too and it showed on his face.

'It would be terribly dangerous,' he said. 'I ... I don't think I could help you.'

'Please,' Timmy pleaded. 'It's my only hope. I have to rescue Katie. I know Mister Carbuncle won't let her go. He'll let the witch keep her.'

'I know that, Timmy,' Mister Needy said. 'But what you propose is dangerous. And it's bound to fail. Your foster parents would never forgive me if I let any harm befall you.'

'They wouldn't blame you,' Timmy said. 'They'd know you did it for my sake and for Katie's. Please, Mister Needy. Please help me.'

Mister Needy scratched his head. He stared at the

ground for a moment.

'OK,' he said eventually. 'I'll help you. I'll modify a can as you suggest.'

'You won't regret it,' Timmy said. 'Now can you get to work straight away?'

Mister Needy nodded and walked off purposefully. Timmy returned to his polishing. As he worked he felt more at ease. His plan might not work but at least he was doing something.

Some hours later Mister Needy informed Timmy that the modification was complete.

'Nearly all the cans are ready,' he said. 'We'll begin pumping the chemical into them soon. At the moment it's stored in a tank that used to contain shaving foam. The pumping operation is fully automatic so we won't have to work tonight.'

'Good,' Timmy said.

'Come with me now,' Mister Needy said, 'and I'll show you what we've done.' He led Timmy over to a can still lying on the trestles.

'My men have done an excellent job,' Mister Needy said proudly. 'Even if I say so.'

With that he pressed a rivet in the seam of the can and a tiny flap sprung open. The opening was just large enough for a boy of Timmy's size to climb through.

'We've built a small compartment at the bottom of the can,' Mister Needy explained. 'Just as you described. It's big enough for you to hide in. And you can also open the flap from the inside. I've also placed a torch and sandwiches and a drink in the compartment. And we've drilled some secret holes in the can so that you'll have air.'

'It's brilliant,' Timmy said enthusiastically. 'You've done a great job.'

'I think so,' Mister Needy said, pleased by the praise.

'I'm going to hide in the factory tonight,' Timmy said. 'So you must tell my foster parents what I intend doing. Tell them not to worry. Once the cans are filled I'll slip into the compartment. Then tomorrow I'll get to the North Pole. Once there I'll try and rescue Katie.'

'I hope you do rescue her,' Mister Needy said. 'Now I'd best get this can down to the filling area.'

Timmy slipped away and hid behind a workbench. From there he watched as the hoses which would fill the cans were connected. Then Mister Vicious ordered the workmen to leave the factory. When they had gone Timmy heard foot-steps. He peered out and saw Mister Carbuncle approach.

'I want to switch on the pumps myself,' Mister Carbuncle said. 'It's such an historic day. I want my name in the history books as the man who destroyed Toyland and

144

became the richest man who ever lived.'

With that he pressed a red button. There was a whirring sound as the pumps started up.

Mister Carbuncle listened for some moments to the sound that was like music to his ears.

'I'd love to stay here all night,' he said. 'But I have a long journey ahead of me tomorrow. I must get some rest.'

'See that the factory is well guarded,' he added to Mister Vicious. 'Make sure Timmy Goodfellow doesn't get in here. If he does he's likely to get up to mischief. Now I must go and have my beauty sleep.'

'Don't worry, Boss,' Mister Vicious said. 'No one'll get in here. I'll have guards posted everywhere.'

'You'd best have,' Mister Carbuncle said and he strode away, followed by Mister Vicious.

A moment later Timmy heard the doors of the factory being locked. He was now all alone. From his hiding place he listened to the pumps.

'If only I could do something about them,' he thought. 'But I can't switch them off. The thugs would know by the weight that the cans were empty.'

He stared about and it was then that the sign on the tank caught his eye. He stared at it and whooped. With a bound he leapt from his hiding place and ran across the factory floor. With trembling fingers he operated a number of valves before running back to his hiding place. Mister Carbuncle and his thugs would now be in for a second surprise when they reached the North Pole. Timmy Goodfellow was certain of that.

22
All Aboard for the North Pole

All night the pumps hummed. For hours Timmy listened to them. But fatigue eventually overcame him and he curled up on the floor and slept. Silence woke him and as he sat up he realised the pumps had turned off. It was time to re-set the valves and hide in the secret compartment.

Emerging from his hiding place, he re-set the valves. Then he went along to the modified can. He pressed the rivet and the flap opened. With a last look around, Timmy climbed inside the compartment and closed the flap.

It was pitch black and by feeling around him Timmy located the torch. He switched the torch on and the narrow beam illuminated the compartment. Light reflected off the polished metal in a dazzling display of rainbow colours.

Timmy wanted to keep the torch lit all the time. The shimmering colours were company for him in his confined hiding place. But he knew he would have to conserve his batteries for emergencies. Reluctantly he switched off the torch.

Timmy was hungry and ate some of the sandwiches. Afterwards he quenched his thirst. In the impenetrable darkness his breathing sounded loud in his ears and his heart beat like a drum. Time seemed to slow down and then stop as he dozed off.

Voices roused him and he awoke to hear Mister Vicious directing operations. They were loading the cans. Suddenly Timmy's can was hoisted up and he felt himself being carried along. The can was loaded onto a lorry and was soon speeding towards the airport. There, the can was put onto an aircraft which took off for the North Pole.

That morning Katie Goodfellow was in despair. The intense cold and hunger had weakened her brave spirit and she huddled in her cell. She had slept briefly and dreamed of freedom – of green fields and flowers and warm sunshine on her face. But then she woke to reality.

A manic cackle alerted her. It was Mrs Haggard, dressed in her many coats, hats and scarves. She had brought Katie food, a cold watery porridge with a film of ice already formed on the top. Yet Katie was glad of the food and with a shaking hand tried to eat it. Most of it fell from the spoon though. More dribbled down her chin and froze there. And whenever the spoon touched her skin, it burned like a hot iron. Already her lips were chapped and flecked with blood.

The mess angered Mrs Haggard and she grabbed the bowl.

'How dare you mess up your cell,' she screeched. 'Now I'll have to clean it. Well, I'll teach you a lesson. Come on. Outside with you.'

Katie could hardly move and two goblins had to be summoned to take her out. They dragged her from the palace and threw her out on the ice cap. The wind shrieked down from the North Pole, laden with frozen particles of ice. It struck Katie's exposed flesh and bruised her. She sobbed uncontrollably and cried for Timmy, her thin voice carrying across the frozen wastes.

In their dens the polar bears heard her cries. Mothers cuddled their cubs closer. Fathers paced to and fro, furious at their helplessness. Icy Witch was their enemy and they feared her too much to intervene.

In his magnificent royal den, Whitey, the king of the polar bears, decided to investigate. With a growl that echoed across the ice, he made his way towards the witch's palace. He slipped from ridge to ridge until he was close enough to look down on the black building.

Below him he saw the huddled figure of Katie. Whitey sniffed at the forlorn sight and rubbed his eyes with his furry paws. As he wondered how he might help her, the drawbridge was lowered and two goblins emerged dragging her back inside. Helplessly Whitey turned away and plodded slowly homewards.

The aircraft carrying the aerosol cans approached the North Pole. Below, the red beacon lit by Icy Witch guided the pilot to the dropping zone. When he was directly over the spot he instructed the cargo crew to begin the drop.

They set to work and soon the cans were falling through the air. In his hidden compartment, Timmy thought he had lost his stomach as his can hurtled towards the ground. But when a parachute slowed it down, he felt better. As his stomach settled, he opened the flap and looked out.

The sight was breathtaking. As far as the eye could see the ice stretched in every direction. It was a landscape of ice – of mountains, plains and ravines, of hills and hollows. In the distance Timmy saw the glow of Toyland and his heart missed a beat.

Timmy turned his head about and spotted a black building looming menacingly against the white backdrop. He realised it was the great palace of Icy Witch. It was there that Katie was held prisoner. It was that fortress he would have to breech to rescue her.

It seemed impregnable and Timmy's heart sank. What if he couldn't get inside to rescue Katie? But he thrust the dark thought away and instead began to imagine what life would be like when he and Katie were safely back in Friendly Cottage.

As Timmy dropped lower still he saw movement on the ice cap. The polar bears were emerging from their dens to see what was happening. Nothing like this had been seen before. Already some of the cans had landed and the bears were examining them, shaking their heads in puzzlement.

Timmy was about to land and braced himself, closing his eyes. But the parachute dropped the can as if it were a feather. Timmy opened his eyes to find his nose only inches away from the black nose of a polar bear.

'Aahhh!' Timmy couldn't help but scream. The polar bear screamed too and ran back to join his companions who were gathering around to stare at Timmy.

King Whitey pushed through the throng and he too stared at Timmy.

'Who are you?' he demanded. 'What brings you to the North Pole?'

'Can I get out first?' Timmy asked. 'It's cramped in here and I'm getting pins and needles in my arms and legs.'

'All right,' Whitey said. 'Come out slowly. But don't make any sudden movement.'

Timmy climbed out of the can and tried to stand. But his legs were numb and he fell over.

'The poor boy is sick,' Queen Whitey Bear said. She bustled in and crouched down by Timmy. 'It's OK,' she said. 'No harm will come to you. Come here,' she added, turning to the others. 'Gather round. We must keep the boy warm or he'll get frostbite.'

The bears gathered about Timmy and sheltered him from the wind. They blew their breaths on him and soon the circulation returned to his limbs and he was able to sit up.

'You'll be fine now,' Queen Whitey said. 'So perhaps you might tell us your story.'

Timmy told them his tale. When he finished there was a stunned silence. Then suddenly all the bears began to speak at once. Whitey had to shout to restore order.

'We know the ice is melting,' he said, when order was restored. 'But this terrible plan will hasten that. So we must take action or our homes will be destroyed. Our futures and the futures of our cubs depend on us. We must hide the cans from Mister Carbuncle.'

'No,' Timmy warned. 'Let me tell you what I've done.' Timmy told them of the trick he had played on Mister Carbuncle back at the factory and the polar bears roared with laughter.

'You're a genius, Timmy Goodfellow,' Whitey said, and the other bears nodded in agreement. 'You've saved us all.'

'All except Katie,' Timmy said sadly. 'I'm afraid I've let Katie down. I ... I can't see how I can ever rescue her.'

'We'll help you,' Whitey stated. 'Normally we keep away from Icy Witch. She's our enemy. But this time we must forget about ourselves. Now, you must rest. You must be fit when Mister Carbuncle arrives. Otherwise how can you enjoy the surprise you've prepared for him? And what a surprise!'

At this all the bears laughed again and even Timmy managed a smile. But the smile vanished as he set off with his new-found friends for the warmth and comfort of Whitey's den, and his thoughts returned to his sister.

The aircraft carrying Mister Carbuncle was approaching the North Pole. The Boss of The Underworld was in a good mood. His thugs were singing and dreaming of the untold riches that would soon be theirs.

The pilot pointed out the lights of Toyland. But Mister

Carbuncle couldn't bear to look. He hated bright lights and the thought that they spelled Toyland upset him. Yet when he remembered that Toyland would disappear in a few days his good humour returned.

'There's the witch's palace,' the pilot informed Mister Carbuncle, pointing ahead.

When Mister Carbuncle looked out and saw the palace, the sight momentarily struck fear into him. If anything went wrong he would end up a prisoner of the witch. Her magic was powerful and his violence would be no match against it. He turned away and it was then he saw the polar bears hurrying across the ice cap. And there, in their midst, was a small black bear.

Mister Carbuncle stared more intently and saw that it wasn't a bear at all. It was a boy. And a boy he recognised. It was Timmy Goodfellow!

'Aahhh!' Mister Carbuncle screamed and frightened everyone. The pilot momentarily lost control and the aircraft zigzagged across the sky. 'It's him!' Mister Carbuncle screamed again. 'It's ... it's Timmy Goodfellow.'

'What?' Mister Vicious stuck his face close to the window and peered out. But the polar bears had spotted the plane and quickly gathered about Timmy, hiding him from view. 'No one's there,' Mister Vicious said. 'Only some polar bears.'

'I saw him,' Mister Carbuncle whimpered. 'I tell you, I saw him.'

'Just imagination,' Mister Vicious said. 'There's no one there, Boss.'

Mister Carbuncle looked again. He could no longer see the black shape. With a shudder, he turned from the window and put his head in his hands. He was still in a stupor when the plane landed and the witch came out to greet them. She informed them that a sleigh was ready to take them to the North Pole. But Mister Carbuncle was too upset to travel just then. They'd have to wait until he recovered.

23
A Foaming Carbuncle

At King Whitey's den a plan was devised to capture Mister Carbuncle and his gang. Two bears were sent to spy on the witch's palace and to report back when the thugs set off for the North Pole. The scouts soon returned with the news that the thugs were on their way.

'Let's go,' Timmy said. 'And remember, stay hidden until I give the word.'

'You've heard Timmy,' King Whitey said. 'He's in charge of this operation. I want you to co-operate with him. Remember our own homes and families are in danger.'

The bears nodded and growled assurances.

'Right,' Whitey said. 'Let's show Timmy what we're made of.'

With a lump in his throat, Timmy gave the orders to

move out. With himself and Whitey in the lead, they marched across the ice cap towards the North Pole. Close to where the aerosol cans had been dropped, there was a ridge. It offered a good hiding place and here Timmy set up their ambush.

A bear was posted as lookout. He would warn of the approach of Mister Carbuncle and his gang. Tense with expectation, Timmy Goodfellow awaited the most dramatic moment of his life.

It was bitterly cold, with a sharp wind blowing. The glare from the expanse of ice hurt his eyes and Timmy had to shield them. As the minutes passed he grew more and more tense. Then the lookout gave the signal.

'They're coming,' Whitey whispered to Timmy. 'This is it.'

'Yes,' Timmy replied quietly. 'This is it.' He turned to the waiting bears and clenched his fists. 'This is it,' he repeated. 'Let's go get 'em!'

Mister Carbuncle and his gang travelled across the ice in a dog sleigh driven by Goblin Driver. Timmy Goodfellow was forgotten as they thought instead of the untold riches soon to be theirs. They laughed and joked amongst themselves and jostled each other.

'Mush,' Goblin Driver called to the dogs. 'Mush. Mush.'

He cracked a whip and the dogs' muscles rippled beneath their fur as they strove to go faster.

Ahead loomed the tall flag pole which marked the next spot of the North Pole. At the top of the flag pole the flag of Toyland fluttered in the breeze. It had a red Santa hat in the centre, surrounded by christmas trees. At the sight the thugs grew quiet. Mister Carbuncle began to chew his nails. It was a habit he had when he was nervous. He stared about seeking danger. But everything seemed peaceful.

As the sleigh drew in beside the aerosol cans, Mister Carbuncle jumped off. Here the ice was polished to a sheen by the wind and was slippery. Mister Carbuncle's legs shot out from under him and he fell heavily on his behind. The jolt winded him and he lay moaning on the ground for a few moments.

He tried to get up but could get no grip on the slippery surface. He slid this way and that way while his gang laughed at his antics. Eventually he got to his knees. But as he attempted to rise further, he fell on his face and struck his nose on the ice.

By now the thugs were in convulsions. They laughed until there were tears in their eyes. Then Mister Vicious tried to restore order. He struck the thugs and ordered them to get off the sleigh and help their boss. Used to obeying orders, all of them leaped off at once. But on the slippery surface their legs too shot from under them and they fell on their behinds.

In the melée that followed there was utter confusion. The thugs bumped their heads together. They kicked each other. They pulled each other's hair. Mister Carbuncle ended up in their midst. He was kicked and thumped from all sides and cowered down to protect himself.

The melée might have gone on forever if Mister Vicious hadn't intervened. He grabbed the whip from Goblin Driver who was laughing his head off. Mister Vicious lashed the goblin, leaving weals on his body. Then he lashed out at the thugs. The lashes fell at random and Mister Carbuncle, being bigger than the others and therefore presenting a bigger target, received most of them.

Mister Vicious quickly restored order. The thugs ceased fighting and cowered down with their arms about their heads. There was silence now except for the whimpering of the wounded.

Mister Vicious ordered them to crawl to the sleigh one by one and grab the safety bars. They did this and pulled themselves to their feet. Mister Carbuncle was in pain and was bubbling with anger. He attempted to kick Mister Savage. But he again lost his footing and shot across the ice cap at high speed.

This created enormous friction and Mister Carbuncle's trousers began to singe. Smoke billowed from them and Mister Carbuncle's screams echoed across the ice cap. It was lucky they did for Timmy Goodfellow and the polar bears couldn't help roaring with laughter at the sight. The laughter would have been heard except for Mister Carbuncle's bellows of rage, humiliation and pain.

In fact, Mister Carbuncle might have slid all the way across the arctic if his head hadn't struck the flag Pole. He bounced off the pole and shot back towards the sleigh. There his feet struck the runner and he shot off towards the pole once again. Back and forwards he shuttled, bellowing in pain each time his head struck the pole. Tiny flames spurted from the seat of his trousers as if he were jet propelled.

It was Mister Vicious who came to his rescue. He braced himself, with legs apart, and cracked the whip. It whistled through the air and wrapped itself about Mister Carbuncle's ankle. Mister Vicious held on tight and dragged his boss to the sleigh and helped him up.

The seat of Mister Carbuncle's trousers was smouldering. Smoke billowed about him.

'Fire!' Mister Savage screamed in his high-pitched voice. 'Fire!' He grabbed an insulated bucket of water which was kept for the dogs and threw it at Mister Carbuncle's behind.

There was a whoosh as the smouldering cloth was quenched.

After suddenly being exposed to the air, the water froze immediately. Poor Mister Carbuncle's behind froze too. Now it appeared as if he had a glass bottom. Each time he moved the ice creaked and cracked. The thugs held their noses and mumbled that people with glass bottoms shouldn't eat beans.

'OK,' Mister Vicious shouted. 'The fun's over. Remain by the sleigh until we make the ice less slippery.'

Mr Vicious ordered Goblin Driver to unharness the dogs and make them scratch the ice with their nails. This roughed up the shiny surface and made it less slippery.

'Right then,' Mister Vicious said, 'let's get on with our mission. Release the valves on the aerosol cans.'

'I'm the boss,' Mister Carbuncle cried. 'I'll give the orders. After all, it was my idea.'

'Sorry, Boss,' Mister Vicious cringed.

With a glare at his right-hand man and his icy bottom cracking and creaking, Mister Carbuncle swaggered across to the nearest can. The other thugs each moved to a can and placed their fingers on the valves.

'Now!' Mister Carbuncle ordered and they all pressed the automatic valves together.

Immediately there was a great hissing noise as the cans spurted out a thick white foam. The geysers of foam spurted

100 feet in the air and Mister Carbuncle and his gang stared at the scene in amazement and horror.

'What's this?' Mister Carbuncle cried. 'What's happening? Whaaa!' At that moment a falling jet of foam struck him in the face. The foam went into his mouth and down his throat, almost choking him. He spluttered and spat foam, which went in his eyes and blinded him. Panic stricken, he lashed out, trying to escape the seemingly never-ending cascade.

Most of the thugs were in a similar situation. They too were blind and deaf and unable to breathe. As they struggled to escape, fights broke out. They lashed out blindly and their screams of pain ended up as gurgles, as more foam went down their throats.

In the midst of the chaos only Mister Vicious kept his wits about him. He threw the whip on the sleigh and covered his head with his arms.

'It's shaving foam,' he screamed. 'Someone switched the valves back at the factory. They filled the cans with shaving foam instead of the dangerous chemical. We must escape or we'll be engulfed in tons of the stuff. It's every man for himself. Run for your lives.'

Mister Vicious did just that. He charged like a bull, thrusting the other thugs out of his way. But as he burst from the billowing foam, he saw the polar bears racing towards him. In the lead was a smaller darker figure.

'Goodfellow!' Mister Vicious spoke the name with dread. 'He's outwitted us. It was he who switched the valves. We're ruined. It's all over. I'll be sent back to prison.'

Terrified at this, his only thought now was to escape. He turned and took to his heels. Timmy Goodfellow called a warning to stop. But Mister Vicious ignored it.

Timmy did not hesitate. He ran to the sleigh and grabbed the whip. He whirled it above his head and with a flick of his wrist, sent it snaking through the air. The tip wrapped itself around Mister Vicious' ankle and he crashed onto the ice. Slowly, Timmy hauled him back to the sleigh. Here, a polar bear took charge of him. The bear cuffed the thug with his paw and Mister Vicious cowered down, pleading for mercy.

By now the cans were almost empty and there was a mountain of shaving foam piled up on the ice. From the midst of this mountain there could be heard grunts, groans and pleas for mercy. Now and then a head stuck out of the foam and blew spurts of it into the air before it disappeared again.

Timmy and the bears watched with amusement. Then Timmy remembered Katie. He had to rescue her. He called out to the thugs who crawled towards his voice. As they emerged from the foam they were taken prisoner by the bears.

Mister Carbuncle was the last to crawl out. After wiping the foam from his eyes, he looked up and saw Timmy Goodfellow.

'You!' he cried, shaking his fists. 'You'll pay for this. I'll see that you pay.'

Timmy Goodfellow stared at his most feared enemy, defeated now and helpless. But he felt no compassion for him. He had made too many people suffer. And he would have shown no mercy to Katie.

'Take him away,' Timmy ordered. 'See that he's guarded especially well.' Timmy handed the whip to one of the bears. 'You can use this on him if he doesn't behave,' he added.

While the bears marched a protesting Mister Carbuncle away, Timmy turned to King Whitey.

'We've saved Toyland,' Timmy said. 'And your homes. Half our task is complete. Now we must rescue Katie. Are you ready to help me?'

'I'm ready, Timmy,' Whitey said. 'We'll do whatever you want.'

'I've got a plan to get into the palace,' Timmy said, looking at Goblin Driver and the sleigh.

'Tell us what it is,' Whitey said. 'And how we can help you.'

'Listen carefully,' Timmy said, and he outlined his daring plan to get into the witch's palace to free his sister.

24
A Surprise for Katie

The sleigh glided effortlessly across the ice as the dogs strained on the leashes. Goblin Driver, now without his whip, called out encouragement now and then. Each time he spoke, the dogs' ears pricked up and their muscles rippled like waves beneath their coats.

At the palace, Goblin Sentry saw them approach and called out an order for the drawbridge to be raised. The sleigh passed into the courtyard and as Goblin Driver dismounted, Goblin Messenger came running with instructions that Icy Witch wished to see him.

Goblin Driver grunted an assent from beneath a scarf wrapped about his face. There was blood on the scarf and Goblin Messenger asked if he was injured. Goblin Driver nodded and was told to attend to his wounds.

'I'll inform Icy Witch that you'll be with her shortly,' Goblin Messenger said.

As he moved off towards the witch's quarters, Goblin Driver headed for the prison tower. He walked quickly, breaking into a run as he drew near. He entered the tower and was met by Goblin Jailer.

'Yes?' he asked. 'What do you want here?'

'Icy Witch wants Katie Goodfellow brought to her immediately,' Goblin Driver mumbled. 'Her brother, Timmy Goodfellow, has attacked Mister Carbuncle and his gang, and his sister must be punished for this. Be quick. Icy is in a terrible temper and is boiling up a great pot of charms and potions.'

Goblin Jailer did not hesitate. He grabbed his bunch of keys and ran up the stairs to Katie's cell, unlocking the door. Katie was huddled on the icy bench, her thin body racked with sobs.

'Come on,' Goblin Driver urged. 'We haven't got all day. And Icy's temper can't be improving.'

Goblin Jailer put aside his doubts. He grabbed Katie by the arm and dragged her off the bench.

'Icy Witch wants to see you,' he said. 'She wants to punish you. Your brother has been causing trouble.'

166

'Timmy?' Katie looked up, her pale face streaked with tears. Her soft blonde hair was dishevelled and her lips and nose were chapped and blue with cold. 'Is Timmy here?' she asked, in a weak trembling voice. 'Has he come to save me?'

'He's not here,' Goblin Jailer said. 'But Icy will have him captured and punished. He'll be locked away here in the tower with you for the rest of your lives.'

Katie whimpered and almost fell. As she stumbled Goblin Driver took her arm and supported her. They moved out of the cell and Goblin Jailer turned to re-lock the door.

'What's that?' Goblin Driver asked, pointing to a corner of the cell.

'What?' Goblin Jailer stared at the spot. 'I can't see anything.'

'There!' Goblin Driver spoke urgently. 'It looks like a file. Had the prisoner been planning to escape? I must inform Icy Witch immediately. There will be serious repercussions for this. Bring the file here. I must take it with me.'

Goblin Jailer was terrified at this turn of events. If there was an escape plan, he was in serious trouble. The witch would have him frozen in a block of ice for a whole week. It would take days to thaw out. And he wouldn't feel warm again for a whole year.

Trembling with fear, he re-entered the cell. But he could see no file. As he stooped down to take a closer look, he heard a click behind him. He swung about and saw that Goblin Driver had locked the cell door and removed the keys.

Goblin Jailer rushed to the door. He grabbed the bars and shook them.

'Let me out,' he ordered. 'Let me out at once.'

'Sorry,' Goblin Driver said. 'But I can't help you.'

With that he took Katie's arm and helped her down the stairs. Goblin Jailer shouted for help at the top of his voice. But the walls of the tower were immensely thick and there was no one to hear him except the other prisoners. They came to the doors of their cells as Katie and Goblin Driver made their way down the stairs. Goblin Driver opened each door in turn and released the prisoners.

In some cells polar bears had been kept prisoner. Some were now very old and had been prisoners for many years. There were snow geese, and goblins who had upset the witch and been cast into prison. An elf was also released. He was one of Santa's helpers and had been lost on the ice many years before. In another cell was a walrus. His bristly moustache had turned grey and he was suffering from rheumatism. Two seals had to help him down the stairs.

The prisoners followed Katie and Goblin Driver to the

foot of the tower. At the entrance Goblin Driver took
Katie aside and allowed the prisoners, apart from one polar
bear, to rush out into the courtyard.

'I need your help,' Goblin Driver said to the bear. 'I
want you to raise the drawbridge. Your fellow bears are outside waiting to charge in and take over the witch's palace.'

'What?' the bear asked. 'Who are you?'

'Go!' Goblin Driver spoke urgently. 'There's no time to
lose with questions or explanations. Go! Go!'

The bear did not hesitate. He rushed into the courtyard
in the wake of the other prisoners. Tasting freedom for the
first time in years, they were rushing about, wild with
excitement. There was pandemonium as the goblins tried
to recapture them. But there were too many prisoners.

The bear who had been given the instructions by
Goblin Driver easily evaded capture and reached the
drawbridge. The guards had rushed off to try and help
round up the prisoners and the bear was able to operate
the mechanism without hindrance. He pulled the lever
which released the mechanism and great rollers began to
revolve. Chains rattled in the sprockets as the drawbridge
was lowered.

Inside the door of the tower, Goblin Driver and Katie
remained hidden. Katie was recovering from her ordeal and

beginning to wonder. She turned to Goblin Driver and caught his arm.

'Why have you helped me?' she asked. 'Don't you know the witch will punish you for this. Oh,' she added, noticing the blood for the first time, 'you're hurt.'

Katie reached out and touched the exposed flesh on her benefactor's face.

'Let me treat your injuries,' she said. 'I won't hurt you.'

With fingers which were still numb and trembling, Katie caught the end of the scarf. Slowly and gently she unwrapped it. As she exposed the face hidden beneath, she opened her mouth wide in amazement. She tried to speak but no sound came. Again she tried but this time she managed no more than a whimper.

For what seemed an eternity she kept staring. Then, as slowly and gently as before, she reached out and touched her benefactor's face.

'Is ... is it really you?' she managed to say. 'Is that you, Timmy?'

'Yes, Katie,' Timmy said. 'It's me. I've come to rescue you.'

25
Icy Witch Meets her Doom

For a moment Katie stood in stunned silence. She could hardly believe that Timmy was here. A thousand questions formed in her mind but she knew this was not the time to ask them. But there was one question she must ask.

'Timmy?' she began fearfully, gripping his arm. 'Is Toyland safe?'

'It's safe,' Timmy assured her. 'Mister Carbuncle and his gang have been captured.'

'I'm so relieved,' Katie said. 'But what do we do now, Timmy?'

'We must escape from here,' Timmy explained. 'I have a plan to get us out. Come with me and stay close.'

Timmy led Katie into the courtyard. All about them

there was chaos. Then, a warning shout rang out as a guard realised the drawbridge had been lowered. But the warning came too late. The polar bears, who had hidden behind a ridge, poured into the courtyard, led by King Whitey.

The goblins were overwhelmed and taken prisoner. Mrs Haggard, who had hidden in a corner of the courtyard, now tried to escape. But she too was captured and marched off with the goblins.

Meanwhile, Timmy and Katie weaved their way to the hanger where Icy Witch kept her flying machine. There was no guard posted and they entered the hanger without hindrance. And there, before them, was the flying vacuum cleaner.

Timmy examined the controls and decided he could fly the machine. He pressed the red starting button and, with a whoosh of flame, the engine burst into life.

'Come on, Katie,' he said. 'Hop on. We must get out of here.'

'On ... on that,' Katie stammered. 'I swore I'd never ride on that again.'

'You'll be safe with me,' Timmy assured her, climbing into the pilot's seat. 'Now hop on before the witch casts a spell over us.'

Taking a deep breath, Katie sat astride the vacuum cleaner.

'Hold on tightly to me,' Timmy instructed. 'Here goes.'

He gripped the flying control column and pressed the thrust lever. With a whoosh the machine shot out of the hanger. Timmy pulled back on the column and the machine swooped over the heads of King Whitey and the bears who remained behind in the courtyard.

The vacuum cleaner shot straight towards the prison tower. Terror-stricken, Timmy was tempted to close his eyes. But he kept his wits about him and turned the control column to the left. The machine responded and banked sharply away from the towering walls. Round the courtyard he flew, gradually getting used to the controls. 'Yaaahhh,' Timmy shouted at the top of his voice. 'Yaaahhh.' It was better than any funfair ride he'd ever been on.

As he circled the courtyard Timmy was going higher and higher. Right at the top of the palace he glanced through a window. And what he saw almost caused him to lose control.

The witch, in her long black cloak and pointed black hat, was crouched over a giant cauldron hung above a blazing fire. She was stirring the cauldron and chanting from a book of spells which lay open before her. Beside her, a black cat watched intently.

'Oh, no,' Timmy said to himself. 'That's the most powerful

book of magic in the world. She can only use it now and again because it drains her powers. I must warn the bears and then get out of here.'

He glanced down to shout a warning. But it was too late. Already King Whitey and the bears were coming under the witch's spell. Their movements were slowing down. Eventually they ceased altogether as the spell turned them into figures of ice.

Timmy knew time was running out. The spell would freeze himself and Katie too. Right now they were moving too fast for the magic to catch up with them. But it would catch up eventually. When that happened they would end up in the witch's power. Icy would then release Mister Carbuncle and his gang and they would attempt to destroy Toyland again.

Timmy had to think fast. What was he to do? How could he stop the witch? He dare not slow down and con-front her. And he could not fly away and leave his friends in her power. What could he do?

With his mind occupied with how he might outwit Icy, Timmy flew too close to the palace walls. A warning cry from Katie alerted him to the danger. He twisted the con-trol column and pulled clear, and as he did so, he glanced back. What he saw made him gasp with surprise. The fiery flames from the engine were much too hot for the witch's magic and had melted the ice.

'That's it!' Timmy yelled at the top of his voice. 'That's it! Here we go!' He put the machine into a steep dive and swooped down. Pulling out of the dive, he began to circle the courtyard. He whizzed around just inches from the icy walls. He circled faster and faster, the jet engine roaring and flames spurting from the nozzle.

Slowly but surely the palace walls began to melt. The great building began to groan and creak, and jagged cracks opened up. From above Timmy heard a scream. He glanced up and saw the witch at the window. She was waving her arms and shouting incantations, her black wand flailing about her. As Timmy watched, she pointed the wand at him. There was a tremendous crack and a thunderbolt shot towards him.

Timmy had only a split second to take evasive action. He swung the machine away from the wall and the thunderbolt whizzed past his head. It struck the wall with a mighty explosion and a huge chunk of ice flew out. The witch cried out in anger and began to wave the wand even more vigorously.

'Hang on!' Timmy screamed at Katie and, keeping a wary eye on Icy, returned to his task. A more powerful thunderbolt was aimed at his head but again he avoided it. It too struck the walls, knocking out a larger chunk of ice.

The witch fired thunderbolt after thunderbolt. But Timmy avoided them all. Slowly but surely her magic powers waned and the thunderbolts grew weaker. By now the great ice palace was swaying. Backwards and forwards it swayed, gathering speed. Then, with a thunderous crack that was heard all over the ice cap, it collapsed. As the walls fell a great wailing cry reached Timmy's ears. It carried on the cold air and echoed across the wastes of the arctic. Timmy saw the witch and her cat fall through the sky amidst the blocks of black ice. In a moment they both disappeared, buried beneath the ruins of the palace, frozen forever.

Timmy shouted in triumph and Katie clapped him on the shoulder. Then Timmy swooped down to land in the centre of the courtyard. The witch's spell had been broken and the polar bears were free to move again.

With whoops of joy Timmy and Katie leaped off the flying machine. They ran to meet King Whitey and the bears and, with the witch's power broken forever, had a joyous reunion.

26
A Happy Ending

The polar bears had a huge celebration for Timmy and Katie. It went on all evening and by the end of it both children were exhausted and in need of sleep. A warm den was prepared for each of them and here they slept all night. When they woke in the morning it was time to leave for home.

Before they left Timmy checked on Mister Carbuncle and his gang, and Mrs Haggard.

'The police will come for you today,' he said. 'You'll be brought back to the city and put in jail again.'

Mister Carbuncle growled and leapt at Timmy. But one of the guards grabbed him and cuffed him around the ears with his paw.

'Sit down and behave,' he said gruffly. 'Otherwise I'll fill your trousers with ice.' The threat frightened Mister Carbuncle and, with a final glare at Timmy, he sat down and began to sulk.

Timmy and Katie now made their way to the flying machine and climbed on board.

'We'll come to see you again,' they said to the bears, who were sad to see them go. 'And we'll always be friends.'

'Take care,' Queen Whitey said to them.

'And safe journey,' King Whitey added. 'Thanks for saving our homes. We owe you both so much.'

The polar bears waved goodbye as Timmy and Katie took off. They flew high up into the sky and turned towards Toyland. As they approached, Santa and the elves came out to wave to them. As they did so an elf ran to a control box and operated some switches.

Before Timmy's and Katie's eyes the Northern Lights blinked and shimmered, and changed colour. Slowly they spelled out new words. Now written across the sky in giant letters was the message: Thank you Timmy and Katie.

Both their hearts were in their mouths when they saw their names flickering in the sky. They waved to their friends below and Timmy turned the control column, heading for home.

ack in the city, Mister and Mrs Kindheart had been waiting anxiously for news. Ever since Mister Needy had told them that Timmy had gone to the North Pole to try and save Katie, they had feared they might never see either of them again.

Mrs Kindheart put on the television to see if there was any news of them. But there was none. Her favourite programme came on but she couldn't bear to watch it. She was about to turn it off when the programme was interrupted by a news flash.

'News has just reached us,' Mister Reporter said, 'that Icy Witch's flying machine has been seen approaching the city. According to the report, the machine is being flown by two children, a boy and a girl. We have no more news at present but we'll keep you informed.'

'Mister Kindheart! Mister Kindheart!' Mrs Kindheart rushed from the room, calling her husband who came running at the urgency in her voice. 'I think it's them,' she said. 'I think they're coming back.' Breathlessly she told him what Mister Reporter had said.

'Are you sure? Can you be certain?' Mister Kindheart gripped his wife's arm.

'I hope so. At least I think so.' She turned and ran out into the garden. Mister Kindheart followed her. Mister

Tom, who had missed Katie and Timmy as much as anyone, followed them.

By now the birds had heard the news and were gathering around, chirping and chattering among themselves. The news reached the ears of Mousey and Ratty and they both hurried towards Friendly Cottage. Already the roads in the area were becoming thronged as people who saw the news flash rushed to meet Timmy and Katie.

At the Town Hall Mister Mayor was struggling into his robes. He was urging Mrs Mayor to hurry as he didn't want to be late.

'Get my chain,' he called to Mister Advisor. 'I can't go without my chain.'

At the home of Madam President things were much calmer. Madam President was always prepared for any occasion. She waited for the helicopter to take her to Friendly Cottage.

Poor Mister Mayor had no helicopter and he and Mrs Mayor sped through the city in his limousine. But as they approached Friendly Cottage the roads were thronged with people making their way there. Mister Mayor's limousine slowed to a crawl and he tapped impatiently on his knee.

Just then he heard the roar of an aero engine and glanced upwards. He saw Madam President's helicopter and began to wail.

'I'll be late,' he cried. 'I won't be there on time. It'll be the ruin of me. Can't this car go faster?'

'I'm afraid not,' Mister Driver said. 'There are too many people.'

'I can't be late,' Mister Mayor continued to wail. 'I'll have to walk.'

He leapt from the car and began to run along the road, his robes billowing behind him, his chain of office jingling and jangling.

Timmy and Katie approached the city. 'We're nearly home,' Timmy said. 'It'll be a big surprise for our foster parents. They won't be expecting us.'

'I suppose not,' Katie said, growing excited at the thought of being home again.

They flew over the city and were surprised to see that it was quiet. There were few cars or buses or people about. They flew on and as they drew near Friendly Cottage they saw throngs of people heading in that direction. Timmy was about to speak when he heard a roar behind him. Six aircraft from the air force flew in beside them to escort them home. The pilots waved and they waved back.

By now the people on the ground were aware of their presence. They began to wave and cheer and the noise filled the sky, drowning out the roar of the jet engines. With a waggle of wings, the escort aircraft peeled off and began to manoeuvre in the sky. Their exhausts trailed coloured vapours and spelled out across the sky in giant letters the words: Welcome Home Timmy and Katie. Well done!

The cheering was deafening as Timmy brought the flying machine in to land in the garden beside Madam President's helicopter. Mister and Mrs Kindheart ran to hug them and Madam President shook their hands, welcoming them back. Just then a breathless Mister Mayor arrived on the scene on foot.

When he heard their story, he gave orders that Mister Inspector was to fly to the North Pole and bring Mister Carbuncle and his thugs, and Mrs Haggard, back to the city.

'Put them all in prison,' Mister Mayor ordered and, turning to Timmy and Katie, informed them that they had been granted the freedom of the city.

Both children were overwhelmed by the welcome. They had never in their wildest dreams expected anything like this. Everyone wanted to talk to them and shake their hands. Mister Reporter wanted their story so it could be shown all over the world. Hours passed before the crowds dispersed and they were alone with their family and friends.

Now they had a chance to relate their adventures to Mister Tom, Ratty, Mousey and the birds. They all sat around in the garden, awe-stricken by the story. They thought it was the most exciting story they had ever heard.

'You mean to say,' Mousey said, his whiskers quivering, 'that you flew all the way from the North Pole on the witch's flying machine?'

'We did,' Katie said. 'It was wonderful.'

'I've never flown,' Mousey said. 'Never in all my life.'

'Mice don't fly,' Ratty said gruffly. 'Whoever heard of such a thing?'

'Would you like to fly, Mousey?' Timmy asked.

'Do you think I should?' Mousey exclaimed.

'Of course you shouldn't,' Ratty said. 'You should have more sense.'

'Go on,' Katie urged.

'Yes, yes,' the birds chirped. 'You can be the world's first flying mouse.'

'I've heard of flying pigs,' Ratty said. 'But this is ridiculous.'

Mousey hesitated. It was a big step for a mouse to take – especially for an old mouse who had great great grand mice.

'Go on,' Katie urged again, and this made Mousey's mind up.

Mousey hopped on the flying machine and Timmy climbed aboard. With a whoosh they shot off up into the sky. Mousey clung to his friend's coat for dear life. He had his eyes shut tight but after a while he opened them. When he looked down he saw the garden far below. His friends seemed tiny. It was as if they had shrunk.

'Eeeek,' Mousey said. 'I love it. I love it. Do some loop the loops, Timmy. And some rolls.'

Timmy did as Mousey asked and the flying machine twisted, turned, rolled and dived all about the sky. On the ground everyone watched in awe as Mousey hopped onto Timmy's shoulder and urged him to go faster

Mister Tom shook his head. 'I think I've seen everything now!' he exclaimed. 'Everything!' He turned to Ratty and shrugged helplessly.

'I've always had my doubts about him,' Ratty said. 'But clearly he's crazy. I can tell you, Mister Tom, you wouldn't catch me going up in that machine. No, sir.' Ratty shook his head to emphasise the point. But when he glanced skywards to see the flying machine dive like an arrow towards the ground, there was a glint of excitement in his eyes.

Katie saw it and smiled to herself. It wouldn't be long before Ratty was up there too with his friend Mousey – only to look after him, of course. Katie threw herself down on the grass and closed her eyes. The warm sun beat down on her face and she could not remember ever being so happy or contented before.

THE END